SHARED

POWERTOOLS: THE SHIELDS, BOOK 6

JAYNE RYLON

HAPPY ENDINGS PUBLISHING

V3

eBook ISBN: 978-1-947093-35-5

Print ISBN: 978-1-947093-36-2

Cover Design by Jayne Rylon

Editing by Mackenzie Walton

Proofreading by Fedora Chen

Formatting by Jayne Rylon

ABOUT THE BOOK

Aven pilots a private jet for a team of do-gooder assassins, but it isn't until she's shared by two special spies that she truly learns to fly.

Konstantin is determined to get even with his Russian mafia kingpin ex-boyfriend, Levin. The jerk sidelined him, banishing him to unlikely babysitters for safekeeping —a den of foreign agents trying to take down the entire operation.

What better revenge than to seduce the smoking hot pilot Levin craves and rub it in his face?

Levin doesn't care if Kon is pissed. At least he'll live long enough to get over it, free of the life of crime he hadn't had any choice but to live. Thoughts of what Kon and Aven are getting up to every night rile him, though not in anger.

Rather than fight over which one of them gets to keep her, Levin plans to teach Kon how to share.

As soon as he gives the Shields the evidence they need to crush the organization he'd been born to run. But when things go sideways, Konstantin might be his only chance at surviving long enough to make his boyfriend's girlfriend his girlfriend too.

The next bisexual multipartner romance in NYT and USA Today bestselling author Jayne Rylon's fan-favorite Powertools universe. Visit your favorite characters or meet new ones in this interconnected why choose standalone in the completed Powertools: The Shields MMF ménage series.

ADDITIONAL INFORMATION

Sign up for the Naughty News for contests, release updates, news, appearance information, sneak peek excerpts, reading-themed apparel deals, and more. www.jaynerylon.com/newsletter

Shop for autographed books, reading-themed apparel, goodies, and more www.jaynerylon.com/shop

A complete list of Jayne's books can be found at www.jaynerylon.com/books

DEDICATION

I've written around 80 books in my career so far (who's counting?) and dedicated them to a variety of important people in my life but this one...this one's for me.

I don't know if it was the pandemic, dealing with my mom's declining health, having a mid-life crisis or what, but finding motivation—even for things I love, like writing—hasn't been easy lately.

Okay, fine, for a while.

When I sat down to create this book it was with excellent advice from a group of fellow-author friends who have helped me navigate these tough times. They encouraged me to write what brings me joy and to be fearlessly me. A huge thank you for that to Mira Lyn Kelly, Zoe York, Lexi Ryan, Brighton Walsh, Selena Blake, Elena Aitken, Ellis Leigh, Kait Nolan, Katie Lillig, Asa Marie Bradley, Mara Leigh, Annika Martin, and anyone I might have missed.

Is Kon, Aven, and Levin's book over the top sexy and outrageously funny in places? Yup. Does it require some stretching of the imagination? Sure does. But you know what? That's how I like it. And I hope you, dear reader, do too. The real world is rough enough, so in my stories everyone gets to have their wildest dreams come true.

Thank you as always for supporting my work and reading my books so I can continue to dream them up for us both to enjoy. Know that you're always invited into my fictional universe on those days you too need a distraction from reality.

1

The gym door slammed behind Konstantin with a bang. Wearing only gray cotton shorts and a too-new pair of sneakers, he draped a towel around his glistening shoulders. They ached after the roughly ten billion pull-ups he'd done in the hopes of burning off some of his pent-up rage. Exhaustion wasn't enough to keep his fists from balling and his teeth from clenching as he thought of the man who'd betrayed him, banishing him to this gilded prison.

His definitely *ex*-boyfriend, Levin.

Konstantin debated turning around for another hour or two of running on the indoor track behind him, though it would be equally futile in erasing the memory of the kingpin's wicked smirk or impressive bulge from his fantasies, he was sure. Even now, despite everything, he missed that fucker. The thought of the danger Levin had put himself in, without anyone to watch his fine ass, made Konstantin sick. Nearly as queasy as the certainty that Levin hadn't believed Konstantin was worth keeping around for protection, or moral support, or the stress relief brought on by a killer blow job.

None of it had been enough.

From beside him, where she'd been plastered since he'd arrived in America for the first time in his life, Karolena spoke in quiet Russian. "Do you want to stop by the kitchen for a sports drink? I could make some lunch for you, too."

"Since when do you know how to cook, princess?" He sneered at the woman who'd been married—okay, more like enslaved—to Vladimir, the mafia leader Levin had so recently replaced following the bastard's demise. Konstantin had seen poor Vlad's brains splattered on the ostentatious wallpaper of his and Karolena's bedroom right before Konstantin had been booted from the compound in the custody of the do-gooder assassins who had become his jailers.

It was fucked up how people could convince themselves that violence was righteous. He should know since he'd done it too when he'd been part of Vladimir's organization. Stealing a few cars from rich guys to pay for his little sister's nursing education hadn't seemed so terrible. It was all the stuff he'd gotten tangled up in afterward that would haunt his nightmares for the rest of his life.

Karolena hadn't earned his shitty attitude, nor did she take his bait. Instead she offered him a wry smile. "I've figured out a few things, like slapping together a sandwich, since I got here. Come on. You can't run on anger forever."

"Watch me." It pulsed in him with a white-hot energy that kept him from feeling the other, way more painful things, hidden at its core. Heartbreak. Loneliness.

Abandonment. Inferiority. Dangerous emotions he had no intention of acknowledging.

Still, he couldn't deny his stomach when it growled loudly enough to be heard over the foreign chatter echoing from the command center nearby. So when Karolena steered them toward the communal kitchen and dining hall across the lobby from the gym, he didn't fight her.

As they passed the brain of the Shields' operations, with its glossy boardroom table surrounded by videoconferencing equipment, fancy monitors, and big dudes, nervous excitement wafted into the empty halls of the assassins' headquarters. Anticipation bubbled up in the form of drumming fingers on the armrest of a chair, jokes meant to disperse nerves, and glances that flicked repeatedly to body cam footage from silent operatives lined up in tactical gear on a plane displayed across the main screen.

Konstantin gritted his teeth and ignored the tug of familiarity. The Shields' motives might not have much in common with those of the criminals he'd been embroiled with before, who'd been about making money at any cost, but these agents had a lot of what he'd stupidly thought his organization would give him—camaraderie, a place to belong, a higher purpose. So what if he'd also had to hide who he really was and the obviously misplaced love, and lust, he'd had for his commander?

Oblivious to his turmoil, Karolena cheerily asked if he preferred ham and cheese or if he wanted to try some weird combination of smashed up peanuts and jelly as she crossed the threshold to the kitchen. His steps slowed. When a pregnant hush fell in the room full of spies next door, every cell of Konstantin's body recognized the demand for attention.

Well-honed instincts went on high alert. His pulse spiked higher than it had during the peak of his workout. His pupils dilated and he snapped his head around before taking one step closer and then another toward the epicenter of the adrenaline factory he was confined within.

It was all for nothing, though. He definitely did not work there.

Konstantin was sitting out this and every other righteous Shields fight. And not by his own choice either. His badass lover had shipped him to an entirely different country—hell, continent—to make sure he'd been properly sidelined from the action.

"Kon?" Karolena raised her brows and curled the manicured fingers of one hand to urge him into the kitchen instead of snooping on the mission in progress.

Fuck that. If he couldn't play, he might as well watch. So what if it was torture? Some masochistic part of him hoped for a glimpse of Levin. If not to drool over the man, then to at least reassure himself that the asshole was still in one piece.

Besides, the thought of being relegated to his well-meaning babysitter rankled. Sure, she was a familiar face and made a great interpreter when he was too irritated to remember the particular English words he needed to tell the Shields to fuck off. And, fine, she'd been kinder than he deserved given their roles in their previous lives. The truth of it was, though, that as surely as the mafia had forced him to fight to survive when he'd been too young and dumb to know better, they'd thrown him away like the garbage he'd always known they would consider him if they discovered he wasn't quite as straight as he'd made it appear.

He'd just never expected Levin to be the one to get rid of him.

Karolena drifted closer and murmured, "You miss him, huh?"

"Levin may have saved your life, Karolena, but he ruined mine." Which was why it pissed him off that he still gave a shit about what happened to the new head of their organization.

"As much as I hated Vladimir, there was still some part of me that mourned when he died."

"You mean when your new boyfriends murdered him." Konstantin regretted the bitter accusation as soon as it flew from his lips. No matter how hard or how long he'd tried to fit in, he'd never been as cold-blooded as most of his associates.

Karolena spun to leave. He reached out and clasped her wrist gently in his hand. Her eyes flew to him, her lips parted on a gasp. Inside the command center, a chair rolled back from the table as Legend rose, glaring through the open doorway, at the place where they were connected.

Karolena flashed the larger of her mates a reassuring, if slightly wobbly, smile.

"I'm sorry," Konstantin muttered. "You didn't deserve that. Any of it."

"I know." Karolena stood taller then. He wondered at how her time at Shields had transformed her. Maybe it wasn't all bad there. "And I forgive you. If we're quiet, they'll probably let us stay and watch. Sometimes I know things that can help and you have a lot more insider info than me."

Konstantin nodded. He released Karolena and held his hands up, palms out, chest high as he strolled into the command center. Hopefully, Legend could see he was no threat. The mountain of a man stared him down before sinking back into his chair. Tavish put his hand over Legend's from his place next to his partner and squeezed reassuringly without taking his gaze from the mission unfolding on the screens surrounding them. No one else paid either the guys' protective bent or their personal bond any mind.

What would it be like to be able to be that open without fear of recrimination?

Konstantin figured he'd never know because Levin had wrecked him for anyone else. Despite the fact that he was surrounded by smoking hot men in his exile, exactly none of them had piqued his interest in the weeks he'd been there. In fact, the only person who had was visible onscreen at that moment.

A camera mounted high in the cockpit of the Shields' private jet showed Aven with her eyes forward while her hands flipped switches, pushed buttons, and steered the plane. She read descending numbers from one of the ten million gauges surrounding her. Confident and fearless, she navigated the final approach into a private Russian airfield he instantly recognized as a rural drop-off point he'd manned plenty of times when shipments of weapons or drugs needed to be transported.

What exactly were they up to? Taking supplies to Levin under the guise of a more sinister delivery? Or picking something up...?

Konstantin knew why they hadn't let it slip sooner that they were going. He would have found a way to smuggle himself onto their flight, Levin's instructions be damned.

He shifted his stare from the long, strawberry blonde mane of the Shields' pilot extraordinaire, Aven, who also happened to be his across-the-hall neighbor. Instead, he took in the man sitting at the head of the command center table fifteen feet away. Jordan was tall with dark close-cropped hair and wise eyes that had begun to crinkle at their corners. Their gazes locked and Konstantin braced himself to be sent away, yet again.

Instead, Jordan tapped his chin a few times then glanced at his team manager, James. The guy smiled before nodding at his boss. Jordan turned back to Konstantin. He shrugged, then promptly ignored Konstantin in favor of monitoring the activities going on half a world away.

It wasn't exactly a ringing endorsement, but Kon would take it.

Karolena nudged him toward two empty seats at the end of the table, beside the tanned man everyone called Cash. Though Kon had tried not to give a fuck, figuring out the dirt on his abductors was the first step in gaining leverage to break free. From what he'd gathered, he was pretty sure Cash was attached to the group's sniper, Aarav, and one of their female agents, Sola, who could scale the rock-climbing wall in the gym twice as fast as any of the men on the team.

Despite his best efforts at disdain, she—and her guys—had impressed the hell out of Konstantin.

It seemed like they'd also included the blonde medic and the two agents she lived with, Knox and Marcus, on tonight's team. It hadn't taken Konstantin long to realize they definitely had some unusual living arrangements in the Shields headquarters and even the rest of this backwoods town, if the other friends that dropped by on occasion were any indication.

Ruby—their computer geek—tapped away at her station, adding two tiny windows with feeds containing the body cam footage from her boyfriends, Ace and Liam, to her personal screen. If anyone else noticed, they didn't call her on it.

Konstantin knew from experience that running jobs with someone you slept with added both the possibility for deadly distraction and also a closeness that could be a competitive advantage when it came to making split second decisions in the field. It seemed to be working out better for the Shields than it had for him and Levin.

That's because he never truly trusted you. Kon scrubbed his hand over his face as if it would wipe the errant thought from his mind. How had he let Levin down? What else could he have done to prove he was worthy to be used by the kingpin instead of a tool broken enough to be discarded?

The ground rushed up to meet the Shields' jet. Flashing white lights periodically illuminated the landing strip as it grew closer and closer. The wheels of the plane kissed the pavement, which wasn't in the greatest of condition. Even so, the camera hardly jiggled as Aven glided down the runway, bringing them to a stop.

As soon as she did, a flurry of motion followed. Not chaos. No, this was the precision movement of a luxury watch like the one Levin prized. Sola took the lead, opening the door and charging down the stairs into enemy territory, cloaked in night. Aarav was right behind her, a mean rifle slung across his chest. They trotted into the darkness and vanished as Marcus and Knox spread out in the other direction. That left Ace and Liam to greet the small contingent of men waiting on the fringes of the shadows.

Konstantin leaned forward, squinting. He was almost sure...

His guts clenched, and it had nothing to do with the fact that he was starving.

Or at least not for food.

Levin looked like shit. But that didn't stop Konstantin from getting stiff at the sight of him. Great, now bailing wasn't an option, unless he wanted to show the rest of the team what he was hiding under their boardroom table. Dark circles under Levin's eyes and the tense clench of his jaw made Kon wish he was there to help the man relax properly. How long could he keep this charade up by himself?

Konstantin figured it was no coincidence that some of the strongest but not-so-bright men were the ones Levin had chosen to load heavy-looking crates into the cargo hold of Aven's jet in exchange for sleek black hard plastic boxes.

"You're giving him more tech?" Konstantin didn't mean to say it out loud. But he was glad he had when Jordan confirmed it.

"Yeah. We need copies of all his hard drives and camera footage. The more info we can strip out of there, the more ammunition we have to shut the whole thing down."

"And what are you taking in exchange?" Cold hard cash wouldn't occupy as much space as those boxes were capable of holding nor would it be as dense as whatever was in them. Besides, what could they have that the Shields wanted? Weren't they supposed to be different than the usual gun runners?

"Ten men. It's getting too risky to keep them over there." Jordan didn't take his eyes off the action.

"Huh?" Konstantin looked to James instead. What was he missing? The mafia weren't the sort to take prisoners. They were far more ruthless, making sure their enemies could never threaten them again at least after they'd forced them to talk by any means necessary.

"Your guy has been protecting some agents from other European countries who were made. He spared their lives and hid them away instead of taking them out, like he made it seem. He's also rounded up some higher-ups from rival organizations who were dispatched to challenge him after Vladimir, uh, disappeared. They're *very* valuable witnesses. An asset we can't afford to lose," James answered with a wince. Neither he nor Jordan seemed to understand what cost Levin would pay if he was caught. Or rather, the men probably didn't care like Konstantin did despite his best efforts.

His cock deflated.

"He's not mine. But you're going to get Levin killed." Terror and grief threatened to drown Konstantin. It was bad enough that Levin had let him go. It was unbearable to think about him not being out there, somewhere, even if Konstantin couldn't have him.

"Always a possibility in our line of work." Jordan didn't try to bullshit him, which somehow soothed him more than if the guy had been oblivious to the hazard. "But we're doing everything we can to avoid that."

Konstantin shot to his feet and paced behind the table. There was nothing he could do to prevent it from there. *Almost* nothing.

He crossed to Ruby's station and scanned through some

of the alternate views of the surrounding areas along routes he'd traveled on nights not so different from this one. Nolan tensed, as if preparing to stop Konstantin from interfering even if doing so messed up his perfect action-figure hairdo.

"Relax." Konstantin only intended to help. Not them, but Levin. Because apparently he couldn't help himself from repeating his past mistakes. "Let me take a look. I've manned this site in the past."

There would be plenty of time to kick his own ass for his misplaced loyalty later.

Konstantin was close enough that he got a very clear view of Levin's handsome-as-fuck face when he approached the plane and jogged up the stairs to speak with Aven. Levin's eyes widened while he scanned her body, like he often did to Kon before devouring him.

Oh. Really? Konstantin's stomach dropped. He couldn't blame Levin for being attracted to a woman as gorgeous as her, but it did make him wonder. How much time had he spent with the sexy pilot during his own time at Shields?

"You good?" Levin asked Aven, lingering a moment too long to be impartial. When he tucked an errant strand of Aven's hair behind her ear, Kon froze.

Maybe there had been another reason his boyfriend had dumped him. One he hadn't suspected, which had nothing to do with his job performance. After all, while Levin asked how Aven was doing, he didn't so much as make a peep about Kon. Did that seem odd to anyone else? Or had only he been dumb enough to believe Levin had been into more than stretching Kon's mouth or his ass around his fat cock?

"Fine." Aven didn't seem to notice the intensity of

Levin's attention. "Let's get the cargo loaded quick. Something about this crosswind is putting me on edge."

"Are the conditions right to leave on schedule?" Levin asked, staring around as if he could see the wind.

"I can fly in anything." Aven crossed her arms, making the most of her pert tits. Konstantin didn't begrudge Levin noticing, his gaze flicking to her chest before he spun away. "Cancel the refueling. We have plenty to reach the layover where we'll bring our guests upstairs. No offense but I don't want to stay any longer than we have to."

Konstantin frowned as the thud of crates hitting the cargo hold thundered through the microphones. They couldn't transport people all the way back to the States like that. Of course, she'd have to make another stop to get them out and fill up her tanks for the long flight home.

He gritted his teeth, biting down on the urge to ask Levin to get on that plane with the Shields. Despite the errors Kon had made in judgment, he was certain Levin would refuse to leave until he'd seen this insanity through to the end.

It hurt too much to look at the man. To witness him suffering in silence and to wonder who he was going to replace Konstantin with. If it hadn't already been Aven, it might have been anyone else by then.

Instead, Kon concentrated on the darkness. Because he knew the location of the backroads he'd taken during similar operations, he was able to spot a hint of movement on the fringes of the property long before anyone else thought to look for it. He pointed to the disturbance. "You have company."

Jordan frowned, then tapped his comms. "Levin, you have a team to the west? I thought we'd agreed only to those on the tarmac."

"Not my guys." Levin spun from Aven. He leapt down to the pavement, shook his head, then evaluated the progress of the transfer. Four crates to go.

"You'll have to stop," Konstantin said to Jordan. Then to James, "Get everyone out of there."

"Keep going." Jordan doomed them all. "Speed things up."

Konstantin felt like someone had punched him in the gut. He doubled over and braced his hands on his knees. This wasn't going to end well. And worse, did that mean someone suspected Levin wasn't the evil mastermind he'd pretended to be?

Or was this a simple case of an upstart testing the waters after a power shift, looking for an opportunity to grab some for themselves?

Neither was good.

Jordan barked commands. "Aarav, Sola, take out the unwanted visitors. They're about a hundred yards behind you. Across the stream."

Konstantin tapped the monitor, tracing the path Jordan had indicated. "If they go that way they'll be trapped. Look, there are more coming here. Tell your sniper to circle around to the red barn on his right. It's never locked. There's a loft he'll be able to pick anyone off from until the jet's loaded." Jordan snapped his stare to Konstantin's. If he was lying, people would die. Their agents. His ex-lover. But he wasn't and if they didn't listen to him in the next few seconds, the gap would close. "I swear on Levin's safety."

Jordan tapped the comm at his ear and directed the team. "Change of plans. That route won't work. Go through the barn. Aarav, you can set up in the loft and pick them off as they cross the runway."

Sparks tingled in Konstantin's veins. He'd be lying if he said he hadn't missed this, the same rush he'd only ever gotten from a good, hard fuck or fight. And since it seemed like the first source of his highs was going to be in short supply in the near future, maybe he could contribute to the Shields. Not because he thought there was a future for him and Levin, he promised himself. Rather because it was the least he could do to make up for the shit he'd gotten too deep in to back out of when he realized he was hurting more than other bad guys.

The pop of gunshots rang through the otherwise silent command center.

Konstantin braced himself. It wasn't Levin who fell to the ground covered in blood, though it easily could have been if Kon hadn't spotted the rogue attackers. Instead, bodies dropped on the edges of the airstrip.

"Go inside! Get ready to take off!" Levin shouted to Aven, though she was already in motion. She bolted so fast that she clipped the edge of her cockpit door with her shoulder hard enough to shake the camera above her. Outside, Levin scrambled to the crew and hefted one of the crates by himself, shoving it into the hold before snagging the largest black case from the Shields. He put it on his shoulder, then sprinted for his vehicle.

Konstantin's stare followed Levin until he disappeared behind the slammed driver's door.

His men followed his example, completing their transfer as the Shields lived up to their name. The agents quickly and efficiently neutralized the threat then ushered Levin's men to their caravan.

Ace slapped the trunk of Levin's car twice as if it were a horse he was goading into a gallop. Tires squealed and it took off, racing into the night. The Shields barreled onto the plane, the engines of which were already winding up as Sola locked the door behind them.

It felt like an hour, but was only a few held breaths before Aven launched them into the sky. Konstantin stood there, statue still, fists clenched and his sore muscles tensed, for the twenty much-longer minutes it took Levin to race through the city to his compound.

Eventually, Levin heaved a sigh that Konstantin felt on the other side of the world. "We made it. No one followed us."

Konstantin sagged, dropping slowly to his knees where he fought for air harder than he had in the gym until James crossed to him and helped him up.

"Thank you." Jordan joined them, clapping him on the shoulder. "My team would have been in trouble if not for you. I know this isn't what you wanted, but I'm glad you were here today."

"I don't intend to make this a habit." Konstantin turned to leave, annoyed with himself for how damn good it felt to be appreciated, and how easily they could use that to manipulate him. Part of him panicked, desperate to be away from the temptation of opening up to them when he came down from the rush of even his tangential involvement when he'd have to face everything he'd lost.

"You could if you wanted to." Jordan backed off, but the offer lingered out there. "We can always use more help."

"Don't forget, I didn't choose to flip sides."

"Sometimes life makes those decisions for us and we only realize later that it was for the best." James grinned at him. "Besides, you don't have to break loyalty at all. You'd still be on Team Levin, just under new management. How else are you going to make sure that fine man of yours stays in one piece?"

"I told you, he's not mine anymore. Probably never was." Konstantin shot the guy the finger then strode from the room, remembering the steamy stare Levin had leveled at Aven.

For the first time since Konstantin had arrived, Karolena wasn't close on his heels.

Had he earned a bit of the Shields' trust? A little more freedom? He hoped so.

It would make it easier to escape.

2

Aven didn't mean to eavesdrop. After all, she was a pilot, not one of the superspies she lived and worked with. It was just that she was zombified after two transatlantic flights, a refueling pit stop where they'd also unboxed and moved their human cargo to the cabin, and—last but not least—an ambush. That unwelcome surprise had boosted the high she always got from flying, though it multiplied the crash afterward too. When she'd gotten confirmation from Levin that he'd escaped, she'd fought not to deflate with relief, holding herself together for hours afterward.

She trudged down the stairs from the helipad on the roof of the Shields headquarters, then slipped into the far end of the hallway leading to her apartment, conveniently located on the top floor of Middletown's tallest building.

Until recently, she'd had the whole level to herself. Konstantin had moved into the apartment across from hers a few weeks ago. The same one Levin had occupied during his time with them.

Aven hadn't realized how lonely it was being

segregated from the rest of her teammates turned friends —family, really—until Levin had left. She missed their late-night run-ins after mission planning, even if he hadn't stayed long enough for it to have become a proper habit.

On the other hand, Konstantin had hardly poked his head out of the apartment since he'd taken up residence, acting like the prisoner he accused them of making him. Or maybe some very handsome prince locked in a tower, waiting for a warrior to rescue him.

Except right then he was standing in the hall, chatting with James.

If Aven slowed her shuffle a tiny bit to catch what they were saying before turning the corner, it had nothing to do with the fact that she was intrigued by the guy Levin adored. Of course it didn't. Okay, fine, she could see why Levin was obsessed.

At least on the surface, Konstantin was cute and compact, though probably only by the standard most of the Shields men set. He wasn't bulky or tall, having maybe only a few inches of height on her. But she'd caught sight of him working out several times now. His steel blue T-shirt hid a lot of definition beneath its soft cotton.

"Sorry to bug you. I'm about to head out for the evening and I didn't feel good about leaving things on our previous note." James seemed unfazed by the dispassionate stare Konstantin aimed at him as he leaned against his doorjamb, his bare feet crossed. He continued, "I should have been less of a wiseass about the situation. I mean, I used to be a construction worker and I remember how shaken up I was when my whole life, future, and the foundation of my identity shifted under my feet. At the time, it freaked me out. Now I realize that if I hadn't taken the chance to try something different when it was presented to me, I would never have met everyone here and become the person I was always meant to be. I suspect you're on the same path I was on not so long ago. Things change. It's unsettling, though it doesn't always turn out for the worst. Still, I get that you're probably having a hard time seeing that at the moment because you're hurting."

"I'm not. I'm pissed."

"Sure, sure." James obviously didn't believe that any more than Aven did. She'd seen the look on Konstantin's face when he'd realized Levin had removed him to somewhere far, far away from the action—both the sort that happened in the field and the kind they'd shared in Levin's bed. However, she'd also been there when Levin—a man not used to begging for anything—pledged to put his own life at risk by becoming a mole in exchange for Konstantin's wellbeing. Nothing had mattered as much to him as keeping his boyfriend whole and protected. Hell, she'd wondered what it might feel like if Levin, or anyone, cared that deeply about her. "But you understand that Levin sent you here because he wanted to keep you safe, right?"

"I'm supposed to believe he told you that?" Konstantin huffed out a bitter laugh. "He's not one to talk about his feelings."

Aven snapped out of her daze, alerting the men to her presence by pressing forward past the potted palm at the corner and into the light as she approached them. "Then it should reassure you that he did. He openly declared that you were his boyfriend and that his only concern was your welfare. In front of everyone on the team. And in private with me, too."

She figured it made her a decent person for ignoring the twinges of jealousy that assaulted her.

Konstantin stood straight, turning to face her, gliding his hands down his shirt then the tops of his jeans as if making sure his appearance was in order, though he hadn't seemed to give a fuck about that when he'd assumed he was speaking only to James.

"You spent a lot of time alone with him, did you?" Konstantin raked his gaze over her from her bleary eyes to her purple boots. It sounded like an accusation more than a question.

"Don't lash out at her." James stepped between them. "Can't you see she's exhausted? She needs someone to take care of her, not pick a fight with her. Want me to get you something to eat?"

"Nah. I'm fine." Aven hoped the fact that she had to put her hand out to steady herself against the wall didn't give away her lie.

Apparently it did, though.

"That's not what I was doing. Not on purpose. I'm not that much of a jerk. Even though I worked for some." Konstantin sighed and softened. "I'm sorry. Damn it. I keep saying that, don't I? I'm not used to being the asshole."

Aven snorted at that. "Levin does seem to come by it naturally."

"That's true." A ghost of a smile leaked through Konstantin's scowl. The rueful shake of his head that accompanied it made her certain he found Levin's alpha tendencies kind of hot. Like she did. She also assumed he was used to taking the guy down a few pegs in their private life. He scrubbed his hand through his sandy hair, making it stick up adorably. "Look, it's fucking with me that he sees me as so weak and pathetic he thought I needed a nanny. I'll try my best not to hold it against any of you when he's the one who made the call."

"I think you're letting what's in here screw up your read on this one." James patted his chest over his heart. "You don't have to get in some kind of pissing match with every person under this roof to show us you're capable. In fact, it's the opposite. It takes a lot of strength and courage to embrace your vulnerability. I don't expect you're ready to go quite so far with us yet. We're still mostly strangers to you. I'm just saying, we're a team, and like it or not you're stuck with us for a while. So if you can channel some of the fuel for your pissy mood—hurt, anger, whatever you want to call it—into something productive, it's the best chance Levin has at getting out of this mess alive. Then you can direct your anger where it belongs. At him."

Konstantin opened his mouth, then closed it again, as if swallowing what would have been reflexive denial. He thought for a few moments about James's advice, then nodded. "I'll do my best."

He surprised Aven by ambling in her direction. When she didn't flinch, he approached her.

"Will you give me a chance to prove I'm not fucking useless?" he asked, the dove gray of his eyes softer and prettier than she'd realized now that she admired it up close.

"How?"

"You've both been on duty for a full day, probably longer. I've just been watching weird American TV while sulking. Send James home to his wife and husband. I'll cook for you and help you unwind."

Aven was certain he didn't intend for his offer to sound

so intimate. Plus, she'd be lying if she denied some company sounded nice to help scrub the lingering apprehension from her mind so she could get the rest she so desperately needed. Recharging as quickly as possible was important since she didn't know when the team would need her to fly again next.

Aven pressed her hands to her rumbling stomach, swaying without the wall to stabilize her. There'd been one thing she'd been craving for weeks. "Do you know how to make *syrniki*? I have some blueberries in my fridge."

"Levin's favorite." Konstantin sniffed. "You really did spend some time getting to know him, huh?"

"He was a lot less scary when he was wearing my pink polka-dotted apron." Aven couldn't help but grin at the memory of the badass slinging pancakes in her kitchen.

"I wish I had seen that." Konstantin exchanged a smile with her, though it didn't do much to erase the sadness in his eyes. She wished she had the right to hug him, or that he would accept her comforting gesture instead of seeing it as another sign that she perceived him as soft if she reached out.

"So…" She was legitimately hopeful. "Is that a yes?"

"Who do you think he learned how to make them from?" Konstantin laced his fingers, then turned his hands inside out, cracking his knuckles. "It's my grandmother's recipe he uses."

"Okay. Then I'm in." Aven would be glad to do her part if it meant filling up on more of that deliciousness. Never mind getting to know Levin's boyfriend a little better. She'd been curious about him since the moment Levin had exchanged his own safety for this man's.

"You good with me leaving you two together?" James asked her. "Want me to send someone up to join you?"

"Tell Karolena and Ruby I'll text them in a bit." James would understand that was code for, *if they don't hear from me, unleash the nosy neighbors.*

"Will do." James nodded. Besides, they both knew Ruby was likely to snoop through the security cameras in Aven's apartment if she suspected there could be anything amiss. Aven was glad to know her friends were watching her back.

"Open the door for me before you go?" Konstantin asked James.

"Why? It's my—" Aven cut off when he scooped her off her feet before she could stumble and cradled her to his chest effortlessly, as if they weren't nearly the same size. She didn't make a habit of leaning on people, having learned early on that was a good way to get dropped on her ass. Damn if she didn't instinctively curl into him, though. Probably because of whatever the fuck shower gel was making his neck smell so damn good that it overcame her better sense. Or the heat seeping through his shirt into her ribs. *Mmm.*

She rested her head on his shoulder to inhale more of his scent and because, truthfully, she was dead tired. Her arm twinged as she raised it to encircle his shoulder, though he didn't seem likely to let her fall.

"My pleasure." James grinned as he pressed his finger to the print scanner on her door. As their manager, he had access to the entire building. Ruby did too, but mostly because she hacked anything digital by habit. He held the door wide as Konstantin carried her inside. "Hope your night ends better than it started, you two. Don't do anything I wouldn't."

"James, you're the least inhibited person I know." Aven rolled her eyes.

"Exactly. Good sex is good for the soul. Then again, so is a home-cooked meal and a conversation with a new friend if you insist on being more boring than me." He blew them a kiss, then shut the door. She could hear him chuckling as he waited for the elevator.

Konstantin grimaced as he carried her into her kitchen then kicked out a chair, before setting her down as gently as her very best landings. "Don't worry, I'm not about to take advantage of you."

Too bad.

He might not be as imposing as some of the Shields men, but he was apparently even more chivalrous than most of them. For some reason, that annoyed her. Maybe because she spent every waking hour around her horny co-workers who were constantly sharing hungry stares with each other when she was the odd woman out. It would be nice to be wanted for once. Of course she had to go and get all curious about two men who were obviously hung up on each other. Maybe it would be best if they stayed neighbors and nothing more. "Thanks for the ride. You don't have to cook some elaborate meal if you're not into it. Toss me one of those apples and that'll hold me over until morning."

"If you really meant what you said before, that no one thinks I'm worthless, then let me take care of you. You're about to pass out. You must be starving. Don't they have peanuts on that fancy as fuck plane of yours?" The corners of Konstantin's mouth pinched. Was it because he didn't want to give a shit about her or because she'd stomped on his sore spot?

"More like catering from our friends' restaurant down

the street. I'll take you for lunch tomorrow. It's incredible." She practically moaned at the thought of the flavors on her tongue.

"Then why didn't you eat?"

"Can't when I'm on a mission. Too focused." And too anxious. Not about the flying, never that. Everything else, though... Now that she'd grown attached to the Shields, she was terrified of losing them. Lately, she'd even started having nightmares about some of their near misses and the wounds Kennedy had patched as Aven raced them through the skies toward safety.

"It's hard on me too." Konstantin squeezed her hand. "Even when I'm by his side, but worse now that I can't do a damn thing to help."

She shouldn't have been surprised that Levin had picked a good man. Whether he believed it or not, Levin was decent and honorable in his own way. Both he and Konstantin were. It might take someone who enabled assassins to do their jobs to see how that could be, but after working at Shields, Aven understood that not much in the world was black and white.

"Yeah, okay. Go ahead, care away." Aven rested her chin on her folded arms atop her whitewashed farmhouse table. It had been a birthday gift from Nolan's and Jace's girlfriend, Laurel, who also happened to be James's sister. A piece from the restoration and decoration business she owned with James's friend Kate, one of his special Powertools friends and sometimes lovers.

Having gone from being totally alone, to a node on their intertwined network of friends had taken some adjusting. And now, damn them, they'd made her long for more.

Konstantin flashed her another smile, this one bold

enough to reveal the hint of a dimple she hadn't noticed before. He tucked a strand of hair behind her ear, exactly like Levin had at the airfield before everything had gone to shit the night before. She wondered if Konstantin did it for her sake or his own, to touch the same spot his boyfriend had. If she could be a link for him to the other guy, she didn't mind.

Besides, it felt awfully nice.

He dropped his gaze to her lips for a moment before clearing his throat and spinning around toward the fridge. As if he'd been her guest a hundred times before, he opened it and gathered ingredients, asking her for direction when he needed something out of the cabinets. For a while, she zoned out and simply watched him moving confidently as he whipped up the batter.

When he finished and flipped on the stove to heat up a pan, he looked over his shoulder at her. "Can I ask you something?"

"Like work stuff?"

"Kind of." He shrugged one shoulder.

"Go ahead. If I can tell you, I will." Aven had to shake herself to remember there was more at stake than a meal or even a bond with a potential asset for Shields.

"Where are the people you smuggled out of there?" Konstantin waved her spatula in front of his chest. "I'm not asking for an exact location or anything confidential but...I sort of thought there'd be more people moving in tonight."

"Oh." Aven shook her head. "Nah. They're in a safe house with some friends of ours in law enforcement."

"Then why am I here when they're not?" He tilted his head sideways a bit before returning his focus to the skillet. Sizzles and his lack of eye contact made his question seem casual though neither of them believed it was.

"Because you're even more critical to the success of this mission than they are." Aven didn't have to lie about that. Jordan would have told Konstantin himself if the guy had been willing to listen before.

"How so?"

"Jordan promised Levin we'd personally guard you until this was resolved. It was the only thing Levin asked for in exchange for his cooperation." Hopefully Konstantin would understand, like she had, exactly what that meant. Levin loved him, even if guaranteeing his survival had caused a rift bigger than all the physical space between them. He'd rather lose Konstantin than risk the man's life. It had been a hell of a sacrifice.

"Not any cash? Or immunity for himself once this is finished?" Konstantin flipped the pancakes.

"Nope."

"Idiot." Konstantin shook his head, but his shoulders lowered slightly as if he'd relaxed a tad.

"He seemed driven, not dumb, to me." Aven muttered under her breath, "And hot as hell too."

Konstantin didn't face her, but he snorted. "And he knows it."

"Sorry. Didn't mean to lust after your boyfriend." She was even more exhausted than she'd realized if she'd let that slip.

Konstantin piled fluffy golden discs dotted with blueberries onto a plate. He drizzled them with honey and finished the dish with a dot of whipped cream before setting it in front of her on the table. Aven perked up at the sweet aroma and the sight of fresh, warm food. She sat tall and eagerly accepted the fork Konstantin passed her, their fingers brushing as they exchanged the utensil. When the first morsel hit her tongue, she moaned.

Konstantin sat next to her and studied her tongue swiping stickiness from her lips and her throat flexing as she swallowed.

"I don't blame you, you know? Levin is fine. And, for the last time, that's not what we are. Apparently, never were. Otherwise, he never would have gotten rid of me." She would have argued with him if her mouth wasn't stuffed. Konstantin said something in Russian she didn't understand, but his bitter tone made her pretty sure it was a curse. "At least, I never could have done that to him. So he must not give a fuck about what we had."

Aven disagreed but there was no sense in insisting he was wrong if he wasn't ready to believe it. Instead, she swiped the last bit of heaven from her plate and licked her fork clean.

Konstantin's stare followed the arc of her tongue. She wondered if it was attraction or if he was simply waiting for her to finish so he could clean up after her. She cleared her throat as she swallowed the last of her meal. "Thank you. That was...incredible."

Surprisingly, it was the truth. Despite the fact that having someone baby her would ordinarily give her hives, or at least flashbacks to dark times when she'd wished she didn't have to fend for herself, it was kind of nice to let him pamper her. As long as she didn't get used to it, she wouldn't miss what she'd only had a taste of, right?

"You're welcome." When he leaned in to collect her empty plate, his hip nudged her upper arm, making her hiss and flinch.

"What happened there?" Konstantin brushed her hair away from the tender spot, crouching for a better view as he raised the sleeve of her top. As she suspected, the skin a few inches below her shoulder was already turning black and blue in the area surrounding a patch of angry scrapes.

"I'm not sure. I think I caught it on the doorframe as I ran for the cockpit when I heard the shots, but I didn't feel it until we were somewhere over the Atlantic and everyone else, including Kennedy, was asleep. I wasn't going to wake her for something insignificant." She prepared her excuse for the next day when their medic would give her hell, she was sure.

He brushed the pad of his thumb lightly around the perimeter of the injury. It would be awkward, though not impossible, to scrub it and slap a bandage over the wound if she wasn't beat.

"Let me clean this for you." Konstantin stood, then lifted her again as if she couldn't stagger across her apartment and tip into bed on her own.

"It's barely more than a scratch." One that stung like hell if she stretched too far, like when she put her hand on the crook of his neck, feeling his pulse accelerate beneath her fingers.

"Then it would be dumb to die of an infection that could have been easily prevented." He refused to humor her. "Which way to your bedroom?"

3

"Uh..." Aven wasn't sure she wanted to be alone with Konstantin in her most private space when the aftereffects of her adrenaline spike had left her common sense addled. Not to mention how messy she'd left the place considering no one typically saw it besides her.

He paused, staring into her eyes as if he could detect the truth in them. "Are you afraid of me?"

"No, it's not that." At least, not in the traditional sense. She was kind of worried that she found it so easy to get along with him.

"Then why would you resist someone trying to help you?" Konstantin didn't let her shift her gaze, shaking her when her silence stretched a little too long. Memories distracted her from the man rocking her slightly in the middle of her kitchen, showing the ghosts from her past who'd let her down instead of her current company.

"Just not used to it." Aven shrugged her good shoulder against his superhero-worthy chest. "Been on my own a long time."

"Well, you're not tonight." He didn't say so, but in that moment she thought he might appreciate that neither was he.

Half of her sighed in relief while the other half tensed in anticipation. But the piece of her that longed for the soul-deep intimacy—something more profound than the physical sort—her other friends had already discovered won out. "It's over there."

Aven lifted her chin in the direction of her room. Konstantin crossed to it and flipped on the light before striding into her ensuite bathroom and setting her on the sink. He kept one hand at her waist, though she couldn't tell if it was to hold her steady or because he simply didn't want to let go.

"It's my arm that hurts, not my legs." She rolled her eyes. "I can walk. I can stand."

"Humor me." Konstantin refused to relent. His fingers kneaded her hip as he rummaged through her medicine cabinet with his free hand. He took out a box of bandages, some alcohol, and a tube of ointment before releasing her to thoroughly wash his hands.

After he dried them, he took a few cotton rounds from the organizer on her counter and doused them with the alcohol. Aven braced herself against the chill of the liquid, the sting she knew it would impart, and the warmth of his surprisingly tender touch.

It was the latter that inspired her gasp, as he studied his handiwork up close.

"Sorry." He winced on her behalf. "If I had been there, I'd have shot them twice for this. Almost done with the worst of it."

What did it say about her that she wished he'd take longer? Was she that desperate for someone to connect with her? To tend to her wounds, both on the surface and those deep below it?

Aven leaned back against the mirror behind her, willing it to draw out some of the heat coursing through her as Konstantin took damn good care of her. He spread medicine over the injured part of her arm, then covered it with gauze and taped it up, pressing only hard enough to get the bandage to stick in spots that weren't discolored.

"That should do it." He looked up at her from so close to her arm that she thought for a moment he might drop a kiss beside the covering. "I can wrap it in plastic if you want to take a shower."

"Honestly, that sounds like way too much work right now." Aven attempted to stifle a yawn, scowling when her arm protested. "I'd rather get horizontal."

Konstantin didn't wait for her to hop down. He gathered her up again, and this time she didn't bother to resist. Aven's eyelids grew heavy as he carried her to her bed and held her with one arm as he drew back her lavender duvet. He set her on top of the soft sheet, then ran his hands through her hair, nearly eliciting a purr from her.

"Do you usually sleep with your hair loose like this?"

"No, I like to braid it. But it'll be fine for one night. Unless you know how to do that too?" She teased him.

"I have a baby sister, though she's not so little anymore and I haven't seen her in...way too long. Our *babushka* too." Konstantin crawled onto the bed behind her, making the mattress dip some. He put his hands on her shoulders to steady her, massaging them for a moment before returning his focus to her hair. He took the brush from her nightstand and started working from the bottom up, detangling the long strands where they fell in the small of her back.

Aven closed her eyes and concentrated on the methodical strokes he used, which began to dissolve the last of her stress. "That's *grandmother*, right?"

"Yeah." He split her hair along her center part into two pigtail sections, then slid his fingers into one half and began to plait. "Though in our case, she was more like our mom. She raised us when our parents took work in a fish processing plant in a village far to the north. It was guaranteed work, enough to cover our apartment in the city, but meant they had to stay for the whole winter."

He stole a hair tie from where she'd looped it around the end of her brush and secured the end of the braid he'd created before beginning the next. Maybe he realized she didn't often let anyone see her like this, so exposed, or maybe he was also lulled by the illusion of familiarity they shared in that moment, but he kept talking and she listened.

"After the explosion that destroyed the factory, we didn't even know they'd died for nearly a month." Konstantin's fingers hitched before continuing down the length of her hair. "And although my *babushka* tried to find work, no one would hire an old woman. That's why I took my first job for Vladimir. Steal some rich asshole company owner's car and pay for my sister's education for an entire year so she never had to slave away in a dangerous factory? Take a box to some dude across the city and buy a month of groceries for her and Babushka? It was an easy decision."

Aven reached behind her with her good arm and squeezed Konstantin's knee. Suddenly she understood why it had gutted him that Levin had shunned his assistance. "You're addicted to looking after people, huh?"

"It's all I've ever been good for." He wrapped the end of the second braid, then asked, "Pajamas?"

While she might have balked before, she wasn't about to take that from him—the chance to soothe himself with purpose, even if she wished he'd believe her if she told him there was far more to life than what he could do for everyone else.

Selfishly, she accepted his kindnesses and hoped it comforted them both. "Top drawer of the dresser."

He left her only long enough to open it and riffle through the tank tops inside before picking her favorite, a baby-pink silk with spaghetti straps and a deep neckline.

"Bottoms?" He glanced over his shoulder with one brow raised, the shirt looking more like a handkerchief than a full piece of clothing in his fist.

"Usually just my underwear." She shrugged.

Konstantin hesitated with his back turned to her. Was he regretting his decision? Or trying to play it cool? She couldn't tell.

When he returned to the bed, he tapped her uninjured arm. "Raise this one. I'll take your shirt off this side then work it down the other so you don't open those scrapes again."

Aven swallowed. What the hell? It wasn't like she didn't change in front of the rest of the Shields at the gym or wear her bathing suit, which covered less than her utilitarian bra, in their pool or hot tub. She followed his orders and tried not to sway toward him as he leaned in close and removed her shirt.

When his fingers deftly unhooked her bra, she squeaked.

He paused but didn't pull away. Truth was, she didn't want to be uncomfortable sleeping in it. When she didn't tell him to stop, he took that off her too.

She might have wondered if he was only into men if his gaze didn't stray, unconsciously or not, to her exposed breasts. But when it did and his lips parted before he shook his head slightly, she knew he wasn't unaffected by the sight of her bare skin.

That didn't stop him from finishing his task, though. The air was thick between them as he settled the tank over her and slid the hem to the middle of her abdomen where it fell naturally. To be honest, it wasn't like the thin material hid a lot. Her insides fluttered when he made quick work of unbuttoning her pants, sliding down the zipper, then stripping them from her, leaving her in the baby-pink barely-there tank and her coral lace panties.

Konstantin stared down at her before muttering to himself in Russian.

She couldn't help but grin as she lay down, squirming into her pillows to get comfortable while he adjusted his package, not as subtly as he'd probably prefer.

"Are you trying to torture me, woman?" He turned as if to leave.

Before she realized what she was doing, she reached for him, then groaned.

"Don't hurt yourself." He paused, checking to make sure she was okay.

"Maybe you should stay a little while longer to make sure I won't." What the hell was wrong with her? Truth was, his attention was doing a lot more than the ointment had to salve something damaged inside her.

Besides, he didn't seem eager to return to his solitary confinement across the hall.

She wondered what Levin would say if he found out she was developing a crush on his lover similar to the one she had on him. Why did she torture herself by picking unavailable men to covet? Maybe because it was safer, knowing nothing would come of it.

And that was fucked up.

But Konstantin couldn't know that. He sank onto the mattress beside her, then nudged her over to make room so that he could stretch out along her length.

Aven rested her head on his shoulder, listening to his uneven breathing as she settled against him. When his arm came around her, she sighed.

"Don't mistake me for a nice guy. I've done terrible things." Konstantin stiffened beneath her as he probably thought of a few of the worst.

"We do what we have to in order to survive." Aven had too, though she wasn't ready to tell him about the worst of it, but she could give him one slice of the truth. "And sometimes we just make bad decisions."

"Awful ones," he agreed.

She tipped her face so she could look up at him when she admitted, "I, uh, have a confession to make too."

Aven bit her lower lip as Konstantin studied her guilty expression. His face fell. "You two fucked? I thought you might have when I saw how he looked at you last night. It explains why he pushed me away."

"What? No!" Aven jerked as if he'd slapped her. "He was obviously taken. But...I would have liked to if circumstances had been different. Your boyfriend is hot, Kon. I'm sorry, but I have a total crush on him."

"You're saying you two didn't...?" His hands wandered to her hips to hold her still as he read the truth in her eyes.

"Absolutely not. We helped Legend and Tavish set up an epic apology date for Karolena, hung out and ate pancakes while he talked about how much he missed you, that's it." She couldn't help but cup his cheek then. "Did you really think..."

He glanced away, his jaw clenching, before he looked back, his gray eyes piercing hers. "I was afraid...maybe. And I wouldn't have blamed him either."

She must have been more tired than she thought. Because he'd just made it seem like...

"You're sexy as fuck with that long hair and curves. Soft and...not. You get shit done. Flying everyone around like a machine. I like dependable people. Responsible ones. Reliable ones."

"You're into women too?" Aven asked, genuinely curious.

He left her no doubt when he rolled on top of her, his muscled thigh pressing in all the right places as he brushed his lips over hers, giving her a chance to object. Which she definitely did not. Instead, she wrapped her good arm around his narrow waist and pulled him to her. His cock formed a stiff ridge across her mound. "Not often. But apparently I'm into you."

"And you were still so kind to me even if you thought Levin and I..."

"I never claimed to be very bright." Konstantin scrunched his eyes closed before reopening them and piercing her with his determined stare. "If something is important to Levin, it matters to me. Whether or not anything happened between you, I can tell he wouldn't want you to suffer."

"So you did all this, tonight, for him?"

"Yes."

Her stomach dropped. This was exactly why she shouldn't get attached.

Konstantin noticed her recoiling and cursed. "At least at first, but I see why he's into you. And like I said, I'm no angel. A man can only resist so much temptation."

Aven couldn't help but smile, even if she turned her face into the pillow so it was less obvious that his praise did funnier things to her insides than pulling a few too many G's on liftoff.

Konstantin groaned. "Careful, Aven. I'm not him. I'll never let someone believe I'm not into them if I am."

She peeked up at him, her gaze running from his clenched jaw to the tendons in his neck, then lower, to the bulge in his tight jeans. No way was she going to let him doubt he had the same effect on her. Before she could think better of it, she raised her good arm and laid her palm on his chest. Not to push him away, but to feel the reassuring pounding of his heart, which matched her own.

Then she fisted his shirt and dragged him on top of her.

Konstantin groaned as he sealed his mouth to hers and devoured her as if she was ten times as delicious as the *syrniki* he'd fed her. Aven let him consume her sighs and soft moans as she arched into his hold. They pressed together from chests to pelvises, his weight mashing her into the bed in the best of ways. She ran her fingers through his hair and encouraged him to take more, allowing him to feast on her parted lips even as she flicked her tongue over his.

But when she spread her legs, inviting him to sink deeper into her, he flopped to his back instead. Konstantin drew the sheet over his lap as if that would hide the evidence of his arousal. He breathed as hard as the agents did when they piled back onto the jet after their forays into enemy territories, though in this case he'd very clearly aborted their takeoff.

Her nipples hardened in the night air, which seemed freezing compared to the heat of his body against hers. Still, she wasn't about to pursue him if he'd had his fill, or had reservations about how fast they'd been going.

She liked speed. She liked flying.

But she had no intentions of crashing after reckless handling either.

So instead she used a voice command on her home automation system to turn out the lights.

"Sorry." He swallowed hard enough she heard his gulp from the other side of the bed. "It's just, I'm afraid neither of us has a clear mind at the moment."

Aven couldn't argue with that. Silence lingered and her mind wandered as fatigue fell over her like another blanket. She wondered what James would say if he could see the hot mess they both were. Would Konstantin care if she asked their friends for advice in the morning?

"No one in your organization knew you and Levin were together, did they?" Aven asked into the darkness, her question a whisper.

"That wouldn't have been tolerated, no." When Konstantin blew out a deep breath and pushed onto his elbows as if to rise, she stopped him again, her fingers hugging his wrist.

"Did you ever get lonely, having to sleep separate from Levin?"

"Yeah, it sucked."

"I know. I'm pretty much the only one here who's alone at night." Aven swallowed, then blamed her drowsiness for allowing her to say, "Want to stay? You know, just to sleep?"

Konstantin eased himself down again and turned toward her, lacing their fingers together. His thumb traced an arc across the base of hers, between it and her index finger then back. "That sounds nice."

It did. It really did. Her mind began to shut down. "Goodnight, Kon."

"You know what? It actually was." He seemed as dumbfounded as her by that revelation.

The last thing she remembered was him drawing the covers over them then holding her hand while he studied her from the opposite side of the bed, as if wondering what the hell had just happened between them.

She hoped he'd let her know when he figured it out.

4

———

Levin scrubbed his hands over his face before glaring at the laptop on his desk, which connected him to the Shields' command center. Things had been much better when he'd been sitting on the other side of the world with their agents, pretending that he could be something other than the monster he'd grown into. Instead, he'd spent the past twelve hours interrogating his men and still failed to discover who'd tipped off their rivals.

He wiped his hands on his dress pants as if that would clean the stains of necessary violence from his knuckles. "I can't pinpoint the leak."

His cramped muscles felt like they were in danger of ripping from his bones after being tensed for so long. He cursed, wondering how he'd gotten unlucky enough to be born into a trap with no escape. As the son of a high-ranking member of the Russian mafia, he'd been doomed to inherit his father's role as *obshchak*, whether he wanted the job or not.

Worse, he'd been damn good at it.

That meant he'd ruined lives, profited off pain, and enforced a code that prized strength rather than cruelty, or so he'd been brainwashed to think. He'd allowed himself to believe what he'd been taught from the moment he'd been set into his father's hands as a baby— that the only people who got hurt were other bad dudes playing the same game.

Until he'd met Konstantin and his view of the world shifted overnight. Seeing how someone so decent had been warped by their organization—used as a tool for destruction and domination in exchange for cash—made him realize that nearly everything he'd ever been told had been a lie.

Including how wrong it was for a man to love another man.

Only recently had he fully grasped how twisted his upbringing and values had been and how different he could have turned out if he'd had normal parents rather than a mafia spy and a woman who stayed with him because she was too afraid of going back to being poor and powerless.

Instead of bailing then, Levin had been promoted. He now ran the entire operation, at least for show, yet he felt every bit as helpless as he had when he'd figured out how badly he'd screwed up. Any hope of salvation depended on the decisions he made now and the faith he'd placed in the hands of soldiers from a foreign land. Ones he would have considered enemies barely a month ago.

The only way he could stop another innocent person from getting tangled up in trouble they couldn't possibly fathom until it was too late was to shut it all down. He'd freed Karolena, ended her bastard ex-husband Vladimir, and taken his place as the head of the organization in order to secure protection for Konstantin. Smuggled out key witnesses and managed to divert shipments of weapons from evil bastards he used to consider partners to international law enforcement that would keep them off the streets. But his cover was growing thin. It wasn't going to be much longer before someone realized things weren't as they seemed.

If he had to go down with the ship, it was only fair. But he planned to wreak as much havoc as he could as he went under.

His father had named him Levin. Had raised him to be a lion, and now he planned to take on the most fearsome beast in his concrete jungle. The mafia itself.

The problem was, predators like him weren't meant to hunt alone.

Without Konstantin by his side, he had no one to confide in. No one to relax with. No way to reenergize when things went to shit. Maybe that had been Levin's first mistake, assuming he had any chance of success after sending his most trusted brigadier, friend, and lover away.

From the Shields' command center, Jordan cleared his throat, shaking Levin from his spiraling thoughts. "We've tried this your way. Now it's time for you to listen to me. Let us send in some eyes and ears. You need backup."

Out of ideas, Levin had to accept or die, and he wasn't ready to quit fighting yet. Not until he'd done his worst to the people who deserved it. Those who would gladly pick up where Vladimir had left off and grow the criminal cancer instead of trying to cut it out of the world.

"Okay. Fine." Levin sagged against the tufted maroon velvet back of his ornate chair, which didn't resemble a throne by accident. The damn thing wasn't even comfortable, clearly not made for him. "I agree that we need to inflict as much damage, nail as many of the players as we can, as quickly as possible. Things are unraveling."

And if the criminals who obeyed him got even a hint that he was faltering, they'd tear him apart and replace him before he'd taken enough of them down to make any difference at all.

"See when Aven will be ready to fly again." Jordan nodded to Ruby.

"You *sure* you want me to check in with her?" Their nerdy tech specialist smirked at James.

The other man lifted one shoulder. "Have you heard from her yet this morning?"

"Nope. But I snooped around in the data feed from her smartwatch when she didn't send us a goodnight text last night. Her pulse spiked for a few minutes. My guys were on their way to do a welfare check when it settled. It's been slow and steady since. She's sleeping hard."

"Don't bother her then." Levin shook his head. He'd seen the flash of fear in her eyes before she'd dashed into her cockpit—not even pausing when she'd slammed into the metal edge of the narrow doorway—and hated that he had been responsible for it. He could have gotten her and all her friends killed. Still might. The ones in the field quicker than those back at headquarters, but if they were made, the mafia wouldn't stop until they'd eliminated every threat.

James arched a well-groomed brow at him. The man was entirely too good at picking up on emotional undercurrents everyone around him would rather he ignored. Could he tell Levin was starting to give a shit about not only one but two of the people under their roof in addition to his *sestra*, Karolena? It wasn't like James could judge when rumor had it he had a wife, a husband, and six other lovers they shared. He seemed far more likely to force Levin to be equally as greedy because he didn't understand that not everyone got what they wished for in life.

James smiled deviously, then told Ruby, "I think you'd better put her onscreen. Send her a video call request so we can make sure she's okay."

"Why wouldn't she be?" Levin narrowed his eyes.

Another box joined theirs in the conferencing program. Black but with a plane icon in the center and Aven's name below that. It took several rings, enough that he almost repeated his command to leave her be, before she answered and her image appeared. It was hazy and dim, as if the blackout curtains in her room were drawn.

The shitty lighting didn't prevent him from noticing how the thin material of her pale top barely obscured her nipples or the gentle swells of her pert breasts. Nor did it keep his stare from locking on the deceptively strong arm flung over the strip of soft abdomen revealed between where her shirt had ridden up and the covers had gathered right below the lacy waistband of a sexy pair of panties.

Levin swallowed the objection he'd been about to make because he instantly recognized the faint scar beneath the pale hairs of the wrist on the fringes of the frame.

In fact, Levin knew every inch of its owner's body inside and out.

Konstantin was in bed with Aven.

His boyfriend held a woman as they slept, cuddled together in a comfy nest of blankets and bare skin at the heart of a fortress where they were both utterly protected.

It was a good thing no one could see his lap or the immediate tent in his slacks as he realized exactly what James and Ruby had somehow already suspected—Aven and Kon had an instant connection, maybe even one stronger than the chemistry he'd had with them both.

Levin roared, like the animal he'd been named after, his golden eyes widening at the sight straight out of his filthiest dreams. Except he was missing. He couldn't decide if he was pissed off or merely jealous.

And if so, was he more envious of Aven or Kon?

"Oh crap," Aven mumbled as she angled her phone higher to crop Konstantin from the streaming video. That left Levin to focus on her adorable pigtail braids and the dazed look in her sleepy eyes, one a partner might have after he'd fucked them senseless. "I forgot to text you last night. I'm sorry."

"Seems like you had a very good distraction." Ruby leaned in as if she could detect what had happened by scrutinizing the pixels in the image.

"The best." Levin groaned. "One I could have fucking used myself."

Thoughts of Konstantin and Aven playing with each other while he watched were probably going to result in permanent injury since he was likely to rub the skin off both his palm and his dick as soon as he had a moment to himself.

"Should have thought of that before you threw me out like trash." Konstantin must have grabbed Aven's wrist, aiming the phone toward himself with a jerk so his rage was broadcast straight to Levin's cracked heart.

Jordan whistled low but didn't interrupt. Beneath his breath he muttered, "Superspy leader, my ass. Always the last to know the good shit around here."

Levin hunched over as if he'd been punched in the gut. He should have realized Konstantin would replace him rather than sitting around waiting to be collected like some prize for Levin doing what was right for once in his miserable life. It was a heavy sacrifice, but he'd never deserved the man anyway.

"Don't antagonize him, Kon." Aven blanched. "Levin, it's not what it looks like. I swear."

"Too bad." He forced every muscle in his body to stop clenching from an entirely different sort of frustration than he'd been experiencing earlier. If Konstantin wanted Aven, Levin should let them have each other and forget all about him. For their own benefit. That would keep Konstantin from suffering any misplaced guilt if things went as badly as Levin sensed they were about to. "Because from here it looks like we share a boyfriend. And I probably don't have to tell you how good he is at pleasing his partners."

"You do," Aven insisted. "I mean, don't. But it's not like I know firsthand although he was so sweet to look after me last night. He can cook and he fixed up my arm. Maybe there was just one really great kiss that gave me a good idea of what he's capable of. Plus I've seen him at the gym and I have an imagination so—"

She cleared her throat as a blush raced up her chest and neck all the way to her cheeks.

Ruby bounced in her seat excitedly.

"You've been watching me?" Kon asked, a wicked smile curling the edges of his lips.

How had Levin not realized how starved he was for attention and affection? For someone to admit out loud in front of others how desirable he was? It probably had something to do with how limited their private time had been and the fact that they hadn't spent as much talking as they had fucking in the moments they could steal away from the scrutiny of the rest of their *Bratva* brothers.

Another regret.

"Why wouldn't she?" Levin didn't blame her one bit.

"And you really don't give a damn, do you? Not even if I do this again?" Konstantin rolled onto his side, cupped Aven's cheek and sealed his lips to her. She resisted for an instant as if unwilling to make things worse or maybe to be so intimate in front of her boss and her co-workers, but even she couldn't resist Kon for more than a moment.

Levin had never managed even that much restraint around the man.

Her hand went to his neck, her thumb brushing behind his ear, and she angled toward him so that their mouths were better aligned as they sipped from each other. At least that's how it started. Within seconds, one of them sighed and the other moaned.

They were a good match, an even one, fitting together seamlessly whereas Levin had often felt like an ogre compared to Konstantin and his slighter build.

Their kiss was like a fire—it smoldered at first, then burst into flames.

Aven and Konstantin moved together, clutching each other as they seemed to forget that anyone else existed but them. Levin could have watched them make out all day.

Unfortunately, James's whooping and Ruby's slow clap broke through the spell the two had cast on each other and they wrenched apart, Aven blinking rapidly as if she couldn't quite believe that had just happened.

Levin merely grinned. How could he not when Kon was being such a brat and Aven was reaping the reward? If only he'd been there to put the guy over his knee, things would have been even better. "Nah, that doesn't piss me off in the least. Frankly, how could it when I think she's hot too? You have great taste, aside from the time you spent in the gutter with me."

The pair slipped farther away as if surfacing from a deep dive into each other that went beyond a simple, if searing, kiss.

"So that's it, we're done?" Konstantin lost some of his spark then. What did he want, for Levin to act like the Neanderthal he'd been raised to be? Displaying vicious selfishness, insisting Kon stay devoted to him when he knew he wasn't likely to escape this mess?

Hell no. He planned to do better. Even if it was the last thing he could give Konstantin. Levin nodded ruefully. "She's there, I'm not. You shouldn't waste the opportunity."

"Yeah, it's a shame when people do dumb shit like that." Konstantin glared at him. He took his arm from Aven and—if the dip of the mattress and her pout was any indication—left the bed without even bothering to ask if he could come home.

They both knew Levin hadn't changed his mind. Nor would he.

"Konstantin, wait." Aven lunged upward, the image going blurry and shaken as she followed Konstantin. All Levin could think of was how they'd make up. How this time she could be the one to patch the wounds Levin had been responsible for even if he hadn't inflicted them himself.

"One second, Aven." Jordan captured her attention. "Is twenty-four hours enough downtime between flights? Will you be able to safely make another long haul run in the morning?"

She looked off camera then back to her boss, her forehead furrowed. Was it because she didn't like contemplating leaving Konstantin behind or because she needed more time to recover? "Yeah. I can go then—or even sooner—as long as you send someone fresh with me as backup. I know I usually do solo runs, but I've been training Ricky as co-pilot since we've been getting busier. There's enough coverage for the rest of the flight crew to be a whole new shift. I don't want to push anyone else with that tight of a turnaround."

"Take the full day. I'll make sure you, Levin, and the rest of the team have everything you need to be successful." Jordan flicked his hand twice and said, "Go. Help Konstantin see we're not as terrible as he thinks and that hanging out with us for a while isn't so bad."

Aven bit her lip. She glanced at Levin, who nodded, then back to Jordan. "I'll try."

When she disconnected, Levin stared at the emptiness where she and Konstantin had been. He pulled his suit jacket around him tighter as if that would keep him even a fraction as warm as witnessing their kiss or exchanging a few words—even angry ones—with Kon.

"At least no one can claim it's boring on your side of the law," he grumbled.

"Somedays I wish it was." Jordan pinched the bridge of his nose.

"Liar." James teased him. "You hated being retired so much you started doing this for fun."

"I think it's pretty obvious by now I still had something to prove—to myself, and to Wren—after letting Johnny down all those years ago. I wasn't done yet. And I sure as hell wasn't about to waste all those years I'd played by someone else's rules. Better to get revenge. To use everything they'd trained me to be in order to make a difference on my own terms when I finally got the chance." He stared straight into Levin's soul from thousands of miles away.

Levin nodded. "It's good you got to make things right."

"I'm doing my best to make sure you can too." Jordan sighed deeply. "Don't fuck this up."

Levin knew a dismissal when he heard one, so he disconnected and shut his laptop. The bright light that had come from his interaction with the Shields—and Kon—extinguished, abandoning him to the growing darkness.

A new day at Shields, for Aven and for Konstantin, was the start of a long, frigid night for him in St. Petersburg.

Levin stood and staggered to the window, its panes reminding him too much of the bars on a cage. One he'd been destined to inhabit even though lions should always be free to roam. Breaking loose had never been a true option. Not for him. At least he'd managed to get Konstantin and Karolena out before everything imploded.

His forehead tipped forward onto the glass, the cold of mid-winter seeping into his bones and traveling to his heart as the wind whipped bare tree branches and a smattering of snow across the compound lawn. Maybe if he let himself freeze, forgot about everything he wished fate had held for him instead, he could forge himself into a worthy weapon for the Shields to wield, keeping as many other people as possible from falling into the trap he had always been caught in.

5

———

Life could be so bizarre. Konstantin had been transplanted from an environment that required constant vigilance to survive spontaneous eruptions of violence to one where his most pressing concern was remembering to bring a towel when he was invited to join Aven and some of her assassin buddies in the Jacuzzi on the rooftop of their unassuming fortress.

His shoulders relaxed as he stepped into the hall and spotted his sexy next-door neighbor leaning against the wall in a sleek black one piece with cutouts along the sides that made it very easy to remember what she'd felt like under him in bed the night before.

He should have done more than kiss her, but neither of them had been in the right headspace and the situation was...complicated.

Or at least it had been until he'd talked to Levin earlier and any last hopes that the man gave a fuck flew right out the window.

"Ready?" He held out his hand though he needed her

to lead them to wherever it was they were headed since he was still mostly a stranger in her world.

"Yeah." She smiled at him and squeezed his fingers. "The hot water always gets rid of my stiffness after a long flight."

Konstantin figured it wasn't going to prevent his stiffness one bit.

When she led him up a flight of light gray epoxied concrete stairs to the roof access, he imagined the times before she'd used this exit to leave. "It must be amazing to be able to fly away whenever you want."

Aven laughed softly. "It takes slightly more planning—and permission—than that, but Jordan gives me lots of leeway. Another contract as lucrative as our last one—Ruby shut down an international crypto hacking ring recently—or what we suspect we'll be paid by interested parties overseas if Levin can pull this scheme off, and I might have enough for a small helicopter of my own. Now *that* would be incredible."

Konstantin would love to be her passenger as she swooped through the sky over the city, completely free, not even bound by the laws of gravity.

He was still thinking about it as they wandered to the far corner of the roof. Lush artificial grass carpeted an area bounded by a wrought iron fence with posts that supported a scalloped string of Edison-bulb lights. A few small square tables and chairs allowed visitors to enjoy food and drinks next to a bar that separated the makeshift café from a day bed and loungers that would be damn inviting in warmer weather. They sat beside the hot tub, which brought the heat to any season. He guaranteed the throuples at Shields put the space to good use. "This is sweet."

"Believe it or not, Levin helped set it up for us." Aven peeked at him as if to gauge his reaction at the mention of his ex. "It started out as a spot for a special date between Karolena, Legend, and Tavish when the guys were groveling after doing something dumb that really upset her."

That would have made a hell of an impression on her, he was sure, considering the conditions she'd experienced under Vladimir's rule. Sure, her world had been ostentatious, but it hadn't involved kindness and certainly not any apologies from the man who'd owned her. She'd been a prop he'd claimed and flaunted as a symbol of his status. A gorgeous woman to match his fancy cars and designer suits. One who'd also had the misfortune of suffering his repeated brutality. Vladimir, like Levin, had been forced to be ruthless to stay on top.

Vladimir had not been capable of compassion. Was Levin? Kon had lost faith in that.

"Levin? Do something romantic like this? I doubt it." Konstantin shook his head. It was easier than believing the man could be sentimental and simply hadn't chosen to be with him.

Flashes of memories bombarded him despite his best efforts to repress them. Levin's hand wrapped carefully around his throat—possessive yet tender—as he buried himself deep in Konstantin from behind. How he'd always used a monogrammed handkerchief or one of his silk ties to clean Kon afterward. Not to mention the passionate kisses they'd exchanged until they'd had to sneak out of wherever they'd found to hook up and go their separate ways to lonely beds.

Could Levin have been a different man entirely if he hadn't been slated for a leadership role with the mafia from the moment he'd been conceived? It didn't do Konstantin any good to wonder about shit he couldn't change.

His grip on Aven's fingers tightened when he realized there were already several people soaking in the spa. Every one of them a woman except for him. Something that would never have happened in his old organization unless it was some sort of reward for a cruel job too-well done.

He couldn't remember the last time, if ever, he'd hung out with a group of ladies who weren't either terrified of him or trying to seduce him in exchange for something—money, power, protection.

He slowed but Aven didn't.

"They don't bite," she teased when the tension on their linked arms increased.

"I mean, only our own guys," Sola chimed in, making Laurel snort.

Konstantin's eyes widened as he imagined her sinking her teeth into the Shields' sniper, Aarav, or their playboy boyfriend, Cash.

Even more shocking was Karolena laughing along with the others. If he thought his life was changing quickly, hers had done so overnight, and here she was, transformed. So damn happy. Confident. Involved with not only one but two of Shields' finest, who seemed to adore her.

He smiled at her as he helped Aven into the bubbling waters, steam curling around her tattooed calves. She wasn't delicate, and certainly didn't need his assistance, but it soothed something inside him that she let him do it anyway.

The crisp winter air spurred him closer to the hot tub

even as he took in the gorgeous crystal-blue sky and the army of evergreens marching up the mountains in the distance beyond the dormant golden fields on the outskirts of Middletown. He could imagine how breathtaking it would be in spring or even dusted with snow.

Especially with an oasis like this at its heart. One Levin had contributed to, which Kon was now enjoying.

He shook his head as he turned back to the hot tub. That was when he realized it was going to be a tight fit with Aven, Sola, Karolena, James's sister Laurel, and their medic Kennedy already inside and Jordan's wife, Wren, perched on the edge at one corner. An open coat hugged her shoulders and her feet plunged into the roiling water while she cradled her rounded belly. Her serene smile as she studied the spot her hand rested on convinced him she was pregnant and not overly full from the lavish brunch they'd ordered from their friends' restaurant down the street earlier.

"You did a nice job on Aven's arm, thanks." Kennedy pointed to the waterproof bandage Konstantin had applied before going to get changed.

"Of course." He might have been a *Bratva* brigadier, but that didn't mean he was heartless. Though it would have been better that way. Maybe then he would have amounted to more than a grunt, so easily dispatched.

He stood on the fringes of the gathering for a moment before he decided he wasn't about to freeze his balls off for the sake of modesty or even courtesy. Konstantin straddled the side of the tub, then stood in the center long enough to scoop Aven into his arms and take her place on the contoured seat. Jets pummeled his back and ass, eliciting a groan. At least he pretended it was that instead of the woman he settled onto his lap having such a profound effect on his system. He wasn't sure he was ready to be that into someone considering the last time he'd been obsessed had ended so badly.

He wrapped his arms around her waist to keep her from scooting away, though he wasn't sure it was wise when she wiggled her ass against him in search of a comfortable position.

"Sorry to steal your massage." He knew she had to get into form to fly again soon. Too soon. But she'd invited him knowing who was coming and what the space was like. Hell, maybe she'd hoped he'd hold her. She didn't cut him down or insist he put her back where she'd been so he kept her on top of him.

"Feels only fair that you give her one then, huh?" Karolena slipped into Russian. She nudged him with her elbow from her place beside him. After studying her for a moment, wondering if she was screwing with him, he discovered only encouragement in her bright eyes, which rivaled the shocking hue of the sky.

She had a strong bond with Levin. Hell, Kon had sometimes been a bit jealous when Levin had called her *sestra*. "You're the last person I'd have thought would encourage me to move on."

"I didn't say that you should forget Levin." Karolena softened her tone. "But you didn't see him here. The person he could become, and how much he liked your neighbor too. I'd hate for you to rule out the possibility of happiness in your future and I'm certain he would say the same. You're not so different from me, you know."

"Bullshit. You never forced me to remain a captive back home."

"Well, I'm not letting you leave now. Besides, we both

did what we had to in order to survive and to protect our families. Here you can be selfish. No one has to get hurt in exchange. So take what's offered. Be greedy. Get spoiled. Levin would want that for you."

She winked at him, then let it drop, picking up conversation in English with her friends as if she hadn't so graciously absolved him of any part he'd had in keeping her prisoner in an abusive relationship.

Konstantin's body listened to her advice even if his mind was still processing what she'd told him. He flipped Aven's strawberry blonde braids in front of her and rested his hands on her shoulders. When she looked over one at him and smiled, he began to rub.

Aven gradually relaxed against him, her muscles loosening as he pressed and stroked. The women around them chatted about everything from what their plans were for the rest of the day, to baby stuff with Wren, and their relationships. Their lives were intertwined and their love on full display, never hidden away or treated like a deviant secret no matter how nontraditional their arrangements were.

He couldn't say if it was that or Aven's hums and purrs or her supple body mashed to his that got to him most, but she could have no doubt about how much he was enjoying her company.

Not when his cock was rock solid against her ass.

The possibilities budding during this new season of his life—despite the cold encroaching on the bubble they currently occupied—excited him nearly as much as having her on his lap.

Thankfully, she didn't seem to mind. She leaned into his touch, which traveled from her shoulders to her nape, along either side of her spine, then lower to her ass and thighs before working in reverse. Each time a muscle unknotted beneath the swipe of his thumb or the stroke of his palm, satisfaction washed over him like the churning water.

When he sighed, she glanced at him. "You okay?"

"Actually, yeah." He thought he might be for the first time since he'd been slung over Legend's shoulder and hauled against his will from Levin's side.

"It gets easier," Aven promised.

The way her friends hushed and leaned involuntarily toward her made Konstantin think she didn't often talk of herself. "How would you know?"

"I've been cut loose before." She shrugged as if it was no big deal, but her entire being tensed beneath his fingers, so he concentrated on easing any resurfacing tension as she confided in them. "I was divorced by the time I turned nineteen."

Her laugh was bitter, devoid of sunshine.

"Sounds like you have terrible taste in men. Like me," he grumbled.

"That's what my parents said." She raised her hands then let them drop, slapping the surface of the water. "Even before my ex proved them right."

"They didn't support you?" Sola glared, nearly as protective of her friends as she was of her men.

"Nope. Turned out they were right not to." Aven flicked a bubble, bursting it and scattering the foam surrounding it. "He cheated before we'd even left the courthouse after signing our marriage license. Banged the clerk on the copier when I was in the restroom blowing my nose and getting my shit together because my mom and dad hadn't shown up. He said he panicked. Swore it would never happen again. I realized later it had been a constant thing from the time we met to when we broke up. Just like my folks said, he was too young to settle down. However, they stuck by their promise to me even when my ex didn't."

"What does that mean?" Kon wondered.

"They refused to let me come home once I discovered what an idiot I had been. I didn't have any place to go. So, I stayed with him until he decided I was slowing him down too much."

Konstantin didn't realize he'd growled until each of the women surrounding him snapped their stares to him. Rather than shrinking from him in fear, they grinned at his reaction. Karolena even nodded as if she was proud of his protective instincts. After all, they were each involved with dangerous men who used their influence—and sometimes their fists—in the pursuit of justice.

For the first time in his life, Konstantin thought he might have landed in a place where everything he'd thought made him a misfit—his sexuality, his need to take care of stuff, his desire for camaraderie, the thrill he experienced when he pulled off a heist—actually helped him fit in.

"What did you do then?" Konstantin wondered as he faced building a new life from scratch himself.

"I wandered for a bit until I stumbled into flying. I took a job at a regional airfield with shit overnight hours because no one else wanted it and it included a spot to bunk so that you could be on call for wealthy clients with private jets. Spent hours watching planes taking off a million times a day, and dreamed about what it must feel like to leave everything behind while you were up there. It took years to afford lessons, but eventually I worked my way up, not only getting my license but becoming an instructor too. I grounded myself and took well-paying contractor assignments with Jordan's agency, when he was still with the bureau, teaching and training. But I gave that up the instant he asked me to join his team because I missed the thrill of flying. It's the only time I feel truly alive."

Konstantin could think of some other ways to get that same high like stealing cars, or breaking into safes, or sex with a mafia kingpin. He'd never once kept anything he'd stolen. It had only been about his addiction to knowing he could without getting caught. It was fucked that he'd self-medicated with that sort of fix.

"It's hard to live when you're constantly on guard, trying to guarantee you never get let down again by refusing to take even the slightest risk in your personal life," Laurel told Aven. Konstantin knew she had bonded with Karolena over being trafficked. To overcome that much trauma took incredible strength. The way Jace and Nolan looked at her, even when she didn't realize it, had made him sure they were worthy of her trust, though.

There *were* people in the world whom it was safe to love.

"Maybe you and I will choose better next time, huh?" Konstantin dropped a kiss on the side of Aven's neck and she shivered, settling deeper into his hold.

"It's pretty damn nice to let someone else worry for you sometimes," Kennedy added.

Konstantin couldn't imagine Marcus or Knox letting anything happen to her either.

"It's not as simple as snapping your fingers or just saying you'll let people in to convince your brain it's okay." Aven sagged then, as if she was too tired to fight even herself anymore. He hugged her tight to him, keeping her above water.

"I understand that." Karolena put her hand on Aven's knee. "I think all of us here have had to relearn how to trust. To adapt when circumstances evolved. But that's life, isn't it? It never stays the same for long."

"Fuck change. I liked the way things were," Konstantin grouched before he could stop himself. Aven chuckled in his hold.

"Really?" Karolena knew where he'd come from better than anyone else there. "Things couldn't be any better than savage brutality wrapped in deadly secrets and constant power struggles?"

Okay, those parts had sucked. But at least he'd had stolen moments with Levin to balance it out.

"With my luck, it will only get worse." Konstantin hadn't realized how afraid he'd been that had been the case. That he'd gone from the frying pan to the fire, even though that had more to do with his expectations than reality.

"If you have that attitude, it might." Sola shook her head. "Don't fuck up your future because your past was shit."

He might have asked the women surrounding him how they'd managed to turn their lives around if the honk of an air horn from the parking lot below hadn't startled them at that moment.

A Russian curse ripped from his lips as he tossed Aven to the side and stood protectively over her.

The women cracked up and leveled knowing smirks at him before hopping out of the hot tub and dashing to the chest-high brick wall at the edge of the roof. He followed, water sluicing off of him onto the saturated green of the surprisingly soft faux-lawn.

He ambled up behind Aven and peered over the edge in time to see James bolting from the building toward a hideous neon-green vehicle surrounded by a half-dozen smoking-hot dudes. Several others, who'd been washing the firetruck across the street, jogged over to join them. What the hell was in the water in this town? Konstantin hoped it would rub off on him the more he drank it. *Damn.*

"What the hell is going on?" he asked as he chafed Aven's arms, careful to avoid the sore area.

"Those guys are mechanics at the Hot Rods garage. They're delivering the Jamesmobile!" Laurel put her hand on her forehead at her brother's antics. He ran around the monstrosity, his hand stroking the painted flames on the side panels of the tiny car with giant tires and a black pipe protruding from the hood.

"It's indestructible," Aven told Konstantin. "Or should be, but every so often it gets nearly destroyed in freak accidents and James is too stubborn to let his baby go."

The women cracked up like that wasn't horrible.

"Our friends over at Hot Rods keep fixing it up and improving its design." Wren was a welder herself for their motorcycle sister-shop Hot Rides. "This time I helped with a bunch of structural enhancements to make sure it's crushproof. It's pretty badass, honestly."

"Let's go check it out. Maybe he'll take us for a ride." Sola pivoted and headed for the stairs.

"I doubt he's going to let you in it soaking wet." Konstantin wondered if they were all a bit crazy, but somehow, he couldn't help laughing along with them.

"Oh, don't worry. It's been waterproof from the outside

since the time it rolled into the pond. And I heard they coated the interior now too so it can be hosed down in case it ever catches fire again." Aven's straight face made him sure she wasn't joking when she rotated in his arms.

Her chin quivered as she began to shiver.

Konstantin lifted her, hoping she didn't mind him making a habit of it. He pressed her against the full length of his body as he strode toward the towel he'd left beside the hot tub. He set her down with her feet on top of his, insulating them from the cold ground even as he wrapped them both in thick terrycloth, bundling them together.

"Damn, where are *my* guys?" Kennedy muttered as she belted a robe around her before going in search of them so they could join the rest of the crowd growing around James's car down below. "Nothing's as warm as them."

Aven cleared her throat, then peered up at Kon. "I don't blame her for being jealous. This is...nice."

Left alone on the roof, Konstantin rocked them as he stared into her pretty green eyes. "It is. Thank you for sharing your friends with me. Showing me what life could be like."

"Maybe both of us needed to hear what they had to say. They give good advice. We should probably take it." Aven went onto her tiptoes then, and pressed her lips to his.

This time their kiss was sweet, full of promise instead of revenge or some bullshit attempt to prove something. Instead, it was simply for enjoyment. For the sake of doing what felt right and giving someone else as much as he took.

They stood there, exploring each other and learning how they fit together for several minutes until someone cleared their throat.

Aven jerked as if she'd forgotten the rest of the world existed, like he had. She would have yanked them apart if he hadn't still clutched the towel keeping them burritoed together.

"So sorry to interrupt. Truly." It was Ruby. Where had she been when they'd used the hot tub? Probably still working, analyzing the ocean of data Levin was sending her and making the most of every second his former lover was risking his life to put things to rights. Shit.

Aven had to try twice before she asked, "What's up?"

Konstantin could tell by the look on Ruby's face and how she fiddled with the hem of her rainbow sweater that whatever it was, wasn't good. "Is Levin okay?"

"Yes. It's not him." Ruby was quick to alleviate his concern. Until he really listened to what she'd said.

"Who is it then?" Aven asked as Kon was about to.

"Levin got an email this morning about an ambulance called to a suburb of St. Petersburg. It's still unread, but I've been...*monitoring* his inbox." She didn't have to spell it out. She'd been spying. Verifying there wasn't anything there that shouldn't be going down. It was her job. And she wasn't about to let her own guys get double-crossed either. Fair enough.

Konstantin held his breath, afraid of what she was about to say next, but it whooshed out of him at once when she rattled off an address that he knew by heart.

His babushka's flat.

"Kon?" Aven clutched him, her forehead scrunching as she scanned his face as if she could read what had happened in his horrified expression.

"My grandmother. Is she..."

"Oh shit," Aven gasped as Ruby bit her bottom lip.

"I'm not sure." Ruby grimaced. "I'm sorry, Konstantin.

The most I could find out so far is that they took her to the hospital about twelve hours ago, but when I called they didn't have a patient by that name. I'm pulling up feeds from any security cameras I can pinpoint in the neighborhood right now, but it's going to take me a little bit to figure out if she came home already or hack the medical system for records..."

Aven clutched his hands as the perfect day around him went out of focus.

"I told you it only gets worse." Bitterness seeped from him. "My family needs me and I'm not there."

"At least you've got us to lean on." Aven held him up then, and he let her. "Come on, Kon. Let's go inside and figure this out."

He tore the towel from them, livid with himself for believing even for a moment that he might finally have survived the darkest times of his life if he was willing to soak in the sunlight. "I'll do better than that. I'm going to get Jordan to send me back so I can check on her myself."

"Uh, that's going to be a...challenge." Ruby winced.

"Well, you all seem to believe that miracles can happen, so let's work some, huh?" He prepared to battle, by himself against everyone else if necessary.

So when Aven extended her hand to him and said, "I'll do my best to convince him."

Konstantin blinked down at it a few times before clasping it in his. "Thank you."

He lifted Aven into his arms so her toes wouldn't freeze to the exposed concrete beyond the patio and dashed inside with Ruby following close behind, muttering, "This should be fun."

6

Konstantin's homeland came into focus through the window of the plane during their descent. Hints of frozen ground peeked between holes in the blanket formed by a layer of dense gray clouds. Aven had left the cockpit door open so he'd spent most of his time studying her relaxed confidence during the journey. Even when turbulence jiggled them as they prepared to land, she hadn't been fazed so he was able to blow it off.

He certainly wasn't complaining, since it was a miracle he'd even been allowed to come.

At first, Jordan had flatly denied his request to hitch a ride on the Shields jet when they delivered additional manpower and resources to Levin. But Aven, and—surprisingly—Ruby had pled on his behalf, insisting it would be cruel not to let him make peace with his grandmother after they'd realized she'd had a heart attack. Given her age, Kennedy had confirmed her likely prognosis would not be good.

The final point in his favor had come when Sola stepped forward and promised to personally guard him on his excursion. She hadn't been on the roster for the restocking trip since she'd led the previous mission and Jordan had rotated in fresh agents. Assigning her to watch Kon didn't reduce resources allotted to their main objective. Of course, that meant Aarav had also volunteered his sniper services.

In the end, it had taken significant concessions on his part to persuade Jordan that he wouldn't be violating his agreement to keep Konstantin safe for Levin. When Kon swore he wouldn't make any attempt to contact or see Levin during the stopover, that he would not fight his Shield escorts about getting back on the plane at the end of the very limited visit—no matter how much he wanted to—and that he would join their team as a consultant and informant for the remainder of the operation, Jordan had grudgingly agreed.

Now that they were about to land, Konstantin's guts twisted. He wondered if Aven would yell at him if he took off his seatbelt and ran to the fancy bathroom. Rather than risk distracting her, or getting in the way of the rest of the agents, he stayed in his seat and imagined he was back on the roof of the Shields headquarters, relaxing in the hot tub or lying in Aven's bed enjoying the nap they'd taken after negotiating with Jordan earlier that day.

By the time they touched down, he hoped to be able to pull through the next couple of hours without getting sick. He stood in a failed attempt to rid himself of nervous energy, sighing when Aven emerged from the cockpit and joined him in a corner out of the way of the commotion. He wished she would hold on to him, for a few moments at least, before he faced the horrible reality awaiting him in his childhood home.

"Doing okay?" she asked, leaning into his side and looping her arms around him as if she could read his thoughts.

"You're the one who just flew for half the day." He diverted her attention from his non-response and hugged her back. He gently traced the edge of her bandage. "How's this?"

"Sore, but nothing some ibuprofen can't fix." She stretched it a bit but didn't grimace when she did.

"Good." He clung to her, hoping she assumed it was for her benefit instead of his own.

"You're freaking out, aren't you?" Aven asked quietly as they stood aside to let the majority of the agents loose to do what they'd come for: to try to cover Levin's ass long enough to get the dirt they needed. A job Konstantin prayed they could succeed at, though he found it hard to imagine.

"Good luck." Ace clapped Konstantin on the shoulder as he passed and Nolan nodded in his direction before they leapt from the jet and into action.

"You too," Konstantin replied, but he was sure they didn't hear, focused on their primary objective. Then he turned to Aven and—what the hell—admitted it. "Yeah. It's been long enough that I'm not sure what Babushka will think of me turning up now. Or of all the things I've done since I saw her last. If she even recognizes me. Plus... what if..."

"She's hanging on. At home now, presumably resting. She was released into the care of a nurse with the same last name as you when she refused to stay at the hospital.

The same woman is working a shift that's scheduled to last for the next five hours so you're still good to go." Aven flashed her phone at him. "Ruby texted me."

She reread the messages her friend had sent before looking up at him then over her shoulder to the cockpit, where her co-pilot was arranging for the refueling to begin. Aven turned to Sola. "You have room for one more in your car?"

The woman's head snapped up. "You're coming with?"

"Doing your best to get us fired today, aren't you?" Aarav shook his head. "Is there any point in wasting time arguing?"

Kon said, "Yes."

At the same time, Aven said, "No."

He stepped away from her. "You're safer here in the plane. Besides, the team might need you to take off sooner than they planned for. Remember last time..."

"If that was to happen, Ricky could handle it. Get everyone to somewhere safe and land so we could meet them by car. But it's not going to come to that. Let's go." She snatched his hand and tugged.

He still didn't budge. "It's too risky for you."

"Says who?" She propped her free hand on her hip. "Isn't that why you're so fucking mad at Levin? Because he didn't let you decide this kind of shit for yourself."

Konstantin deflated. It hadn't felt wrong when he'd said it, but he couldn't argue her point.

"Alrighty then, everyone in the car. From the moment we leave this plane until we're back inside it, you listen to what I say and not one damn word otherwise." Sola pointed toward the black sedan waiting for them.

"Yes, ma'am," Aarav responded with a grin. "And later too if you want."

Konstantin couldn't believe that in the middle of everything he laughed. Sure, life would always have peaks and valleys, but with the right support you could do more than survive, even when things weren't going your way. It had been so long since he'd gotten used to losing that he'd forgotten what it felt like to hope.

It was reckless given his situation.

Still, the warmth of Aven's hand in his as they rode through familiar neighborhoods made him realize how different he was inside than when he'd left those cracked streets behind years ago. He hadn't been home, not even for a visit, because having attachments was the quickest way to fuck yourself and everyone you cared for when you worked with bastards like he had. Any weakness could be leveraged, family being one of the easiest and most effective of them.

He did his best not to think about how close Levin was since the man felt as out of reach as he had when he'd had been on the other side of the globe.

Sola tossed a spare comm unit into the backseat for Aven, who popped it into her ear. "It's not a fancy headset like you wear when you fly, but keep that on in case I need to talk to you. It will translate for you too. It's not perfect, but it's good enough to understand the gist of a conversation."

Aven finished installing the device and offered him a wobbly smile.

"Changed your mind? You can stay in the car if you want." He didn't intend to make her uncomfortable.

"No, that's not it. I'm just hoping you get what you need from this." She squeezed his knee as they rolled to a stop in front of a square beige cinderblock building with undersized windows and no frills.

"Me too." He drew a deep breath, then waited for Aarav to open their door, blocking them with his own body. He and Sola flanked Kon and Aven on the way to the entrance. The agents deposited them inside the utilitarian lobby.

Sola held her hand out as if ushering them to seats in a theater. "Ruby says no one's been in or out since the medical transport dropped your grandmother off. We'll be waiting here, watching the entrances. You've got twenty minutes tops."

Konstantin gulped, then ignored the perpetually broken elevator in favor of the stairs to the fourth floor. He'd sprinted up them, two at a time, most afternoons when he'd come home from school, eager to tell his babushka about what snack they'd had at lunch or his favorite animal factoid he'd learned in science class that day.

They were happy memories, if distant ones.

This time he moved slower, filled with dread, grateful for Aven accompanying him. When he got to the door, he didn't bother to knock, instead taking a pick from his pocket and making quick work of the cheap lock.

"I kind of forgot you had skills like that." Aven seemed impressed instead of disgusted, but he supposed in her line of work it was a plus.

He tucked the tool away and reclaimed her hand, leading her into the dim interior of the tiny, outdated apartment. When he reached the hallway to the back bedroom, he called quietly in Russian, "Babushka? Hello?"

It was quiet enough he detected a hint of Aven's comm repeating his words to her in English with only a slight delay. He crept forward.

As he peeked into the open doorway at the end of the hall, he gripped Aven's hand too tightly, afraid he might fall without steadying himself. She didn't let go even though her fingers must have ached. A pair of frail legs made a too-small lump under the clean but threadbare covers. One final step and he caught sight of her still, ashen face. "Babushka? Can you hear me? It's—"

"Konstantin." His grandmother's eyes fluttered open, the once-blue of them overlaid with a hazy white that still somehow shone in the lamp light. "Is it really you?"

"Babushka." He crossed to the bed and perched on the edge, finally letting Aven's hand go so that he could smooth the silver hair from the deep grooves etched on her forehead. It was a shock to see her like this, elderly, though he'd celebrated her birthday every year he'd been away. Her breathing was shallow and her fingers trembled when she lifted her hand to his cheek as if she couldn't believe he was actually there.

Aven sniffled in the background as she observed their reunion. Their connection was quiet yet powerful, one time and distance hadn't diminished in the least. It was as if he'd never left.

"If I'd known you'd come, I'd have gotten sick sooner." She patted his face before letting her arm rest at her side as if that was all the energy she had left.

"I'm sorry," he whispered. "It wasn't safe before."

"And it is now?" His grandmother searched his eyes as if she could look through them to read his soul-deep regrets before her gaze wandered to Aven. "What's different? I'll die happy if you tell me something's changed."

Konstantin looked over his shoulder in the same

direction, his stare locking with Aven's for a moment. A calm came over him, erasing some of his distress. "It has."

Aven waved adorably to Babushka, who obviously loved Kon more than he deserved. Was she wondering what it would be like if her own family welcomed her so generously? Konstantin vowed to himself right then, he would make her part of his instead.

"Good." Babushka sighed. "You're grown now. Look at you, so handsome. It's time you quit running around like a kid who hasn't been raised well, causing trouble, especially for yourself."

"You did everything right. We both did the best we could for Inessa. It was the only way..."

"I know. I know. They were hard decisions. But your sister is a nurse now. She'll take care of me, and when I don't need her anymore, she'll be fine on her own. She's smart and hardworking and grateful for all you gave us. You, though...I've worried so much for you."

"Don't. I'm good." He smoothed her nightgown over her shoulder. "Or at least I think I will be soon."

"With her?" Babushka seemed startled.

There was so much Kon would have liked to say if Aven's translator hadn't been running right then, but Babushka had always known what was on his mind. And what was in his heart. "Uh, we just met, but she gives me hope."

"This is wonderful. Everything I wished came true." She smiled softly. "I didn't think you were the marrying type."

He couldn't tell if that meant she'd suspected he was attracted to men. It was something he hadn't fully accepted about himself until after he'd left.

Konstantin braced himself in case things went

sideways, but instead his grandmother continued, "All I've ever wanted was for you to be happy. And free. No matter what that looked like."

"I'm not any good at being normal." He couldn't say he regretted that either.

"You're perfect. I've always loved you exactly as you are."

"I love you too, Babushka."

His grandmother began to fade, her voice reduced to a murmur. "You're not staying, are you?"

Konstantin swallowed hard, then shook his head.

Before they could say their final goodbyes, or simply sit in silence for the last few minutes he had with her, Sola chirped over the radio. "Son of a bitch! We've got a problem."

Kon leapt to his feet and faced the door, shoving Aven behind him.

"He always takes care of those who are important to him." His grandmother sounded proud.

"What's wrong?" Aven asked Sola.

"Levin just blew past us and is sprinting up the stairs. We could have stopped him but we didn't want to hurt him or draw attention. You'd better open the door for him or he's going to break the thing down." Sola cursed again. "Who the fuck told him we were coming?"

Aven whipped her stare to Konstantin. He shook his head no. She'd been with him every minute since he'd learned of the emergency. When would he have done that? And why, considering Levin didn't want him there any more than Jordan had at first?

"Not us," Aven said to her friend as she dashed for the entrance barely in time to let Levin in.

Konstantin stayed put. He heard Levin stalking closer

down the hall like the lion whose name he bore. He'd often talked about getting one tattooed across the wide expanse of his chest. Kon could picture him wearing it over his muscles as Levin locked his fierce golden stare on Konstantin.

His babushka knew who Levin was; everyone in five hundred miles of the city did. And to her credit, she charmed even the head of the mafia when she cooed, "Are those for me?"

Konstantin only realized then that Levin was strangling the stems of a lush bouquet of crimson poppies, his grandmother's favorite flowers, as his nostrils flared and his chest heaved beneath his crisp, icy blue shirt and tailored jacket. How the hell had he remembered that? And why did he have to look so damn good in that suit?

Aven rescued the flowers from Levin's clutches and arranged them in an antique pitcher on the dresser before turning back to the men.

Konstantin and Levin faced each other, not more than five feet separating them. Staring. Breathing roughly. Each of them frozen in place.

He squashed the urge to fling himself at Levin. To crush them together and beg him never to let go. He had some pride—though not much—left, after all.

"Mr. Federov." Babushka's stern tone reminded Konstantin of occasions when he'd been caught sneaking too many sweets before dinner. "Your gift is lovely, but this old woman has one simple request. Let my grandson go. He's done enough for you."

"You're right, he has." Levin didn't take his eyes from Konstantin, not even long enough to blink. "That's precisely why I sent him far away, and came to visit his ill grandmother in his place when I thought he couldn't make it. It's also why someone's going to need to tell me, *right now*, why he's still here with our mutual friend where people who hate me could easily hurt them both."

In the midst of everything, Konstantin was both impressed that Levin didn't roar his response and terrified of the steel in his command. He'd never truly seen the man angry before though he'd seen him deadly plenty of times.

"Oh." Babushka smiled before closing her eyes, as if at peace. "In that case, I'm tired. See yourselves out."

Aven gripped Levin's elbow to keep him at bay while Konstantin plucked a poppy blossom from the bouquet. He returned to his grandmother's side, tucked it into her hair, kissed her forehead tenderly, and told her again how much he loved her.

"Take care of *yourself*, Konstantin. It's time you did that."

He kept it together long enough to promise, "I will."

Even if that meant armoring his heart so he didn't allow Levin's sweet gesture to snuff out his own righteous fury over being underestimated. He refused to be treated like another disposable pawn in the kingpin's war games.

Konstantin brushed past Levin, their shoulders colliding as he slammed the guy out of his way and stormed toward the front door of the apartment. As he did, Sola spoke into his and Aven's ears. "It's been ten minutes. You almost done?"

Kon might have said yes but before he reached the exit, Levin fisted the back of his collar in his huge hand then dragged him and Aven both into the room on the other side of the kitchen, which Kon and his sister had shared as kids. Levin locked them inside it before shoving Konstantin against the door hard enough for the impact to pierce his shock, rage, and devastation.

"What the fuck are you doing here?" Levin snarled.

7

"Sola, we're going to need another fifteen minutes, please." Aven prayed Konstantin and Levin could hash things out instead of tearing each other apart if she refereed.

"Nope. The twenty you had was absolute max. Nine and a half left." Sola didn't sound happy about that either. "The rest of the team is at the storage facility, picking up the diverted weapons Levin left for them. The new arrivals have dispersed. The sooner we get the hell out of here, the better for everyone. Levin included. Jordan is also aware you're not onboard the jet. He's not pleased."

"We'll be out in ten."

"Nine. And damn straight you will be or you'll be walking home."

Aven stepped up to the men. She put one hand on each of their heaving chests. "Don't waste these precious seconds arguing when you both know what you desire most. Each other."

Konstantin's eyes welled.

83

Apparently the sight stabbed Levin's heart as brutally as it did hers. He automatically reached for Konstantin, cupping his face in his hands. He used his thumbs to swipe tears from Kon's cheeks before they could truly fall, unable and unwilling to watch him suffer without soothing him as best as he was able.

"I'm so sorry about your grandmother," Levin murmured. When Konstantin didn't smack his hands or shove him off, he doubled down. "But don't you dare pretend like this could possibly be some sort of act. Like everything we've shared hasn't been the real thing."

Levin got right in Konstantin's face. Aven inched closer as if there was anything she could do to stop him if he chose violence. "Not when my whole world turned from black-and-white to color the instant I saw you again, twice as vivid since you brought Aven with you."

Konstantin still didn't respond. Another pair of tears dotted the corners of his eyes.

"Fuck, Kon. My decision had nothing to do with you or anything you're lacking and everything to do with me. Don't you see how weak you make me? How easily distracted? I'm worse than I thought, giving in to temptation this easily. I should leave right now, let you despise me for your own good, but I can't resist showing you how much I've missed you. How could you doubt it? How?" Levin lowered his hands to Kon's shoulders and shook him.

Aven nearly objected to his rough treatment until she realized Konstantin and Levin were drifting toward each other as if pulled by some cosmic force. They were unable to resist it, or each other. She probably should have left them alone, but she didn't dare interfere and ruin the moment. Or at least that's what she told herself as she stood rooted to the uneven plank flooring and gawked at their mouths as they reconnected.

Konstantin's sigh and Levin's groan reverberated through her, making her both envious and profoundly lonely. They were close enough she could have touched them. Even if she had intruded, she wouldn't have the same kind of bond. Their physical connection acted as a conduit for so much more.

With nowhere for Kon to retreat, Levin advanced, trapping the other man with the full length of his body. Konstantin's arms rose and clutched Levin as if he were a buoy keeping Kon afloat in a tumultuous sea.

They ate at each other, not at all gentle or timid but with the desperation and bone-deep relief of someone who thought they'd lost something priceless for good only for it to turn up months later where they least expected to find it. Levin's fingers stroked the light stubble on Konstantin's face as if the prickle grounded him.

When their bodies began to move in sync, grinding against each other from shoulders to pelvises, it was far too easy for her to imagine what it would have been like to watch them in bed together, naked, as they prepared to blow each other's minds.

Though she didn't mean to, Aven must have made some sound. Either a moan, since the sight of them soaked her panties or maybe a whimper, because it tore a hole in her heart to know she'd never experienced that sort of intensity or intimacy...and maybe never would.

Konstantin had been made for Levin. Not her. And fooling herself about the closeness that had appeared to be developing between them would only result in her crashing and burning before long.

Nothing she had with him—flirtatious attraction or friendship—could replace this for him.

She reached for the doorknob, though it would probably snap off before the door opened under their weight. Konstantin flung his hand out and clasped her wrist, preventing her from even attempting to leave them alone.

Levin did the same, each of them holding one of her arms, including her in the circuit their desire formed as it arced between them. Her eyes widened as their focus shifted to her. Still, she shook her head. "Let me go. I'm not about to be responsible for screwing this up."

"You won't. You *can't*." Levin's insistence only drove the spike through her chest deeper because it was obvious it was true. Their link was unbreakable.

"I don't know about that," Konstantin rasped. "I'm insanely attracted to her. Could easily become obsessed with her pretty tits and softness. Meanwhile, you're a manipulative, hard-headed bastard who cared so little that you let me go."

"You've got most of it right. Except for the bit where you think I don't give a shit." Levin bit Konstantin's shoulder.

"You didn't seem to mind when you caught me in her bed."

Aven had never wished she could fly away as badly as she did right then. Had Konstantin simply been using her to lash out at Levin? To make him regret what he'd sacrificed?

Levin's stare shifted from Kon's parted lips and his face flushed with anger. Instead his gaze cut to her pained expression. "There's no reason for me to be jealous."

Konstantin squirmed then, shoving fruitlessly against Levin's bulky shoulders. He couldn't budge the other man despite the endless hours he put in at the gym. "Why not? Because you never cared about me except to make sure you had someone to plow every night? Me, her, anyone will do so long as you get off? Which of your soldiers is on cock-sucking duty now?"

"Stop, Kon. You're still the only man I've ever slept with."

"Fine, then how many mafia fangirls have you had in your bed since you kicked me out of it?"

Levin raked his teeth down his lover's neck as his free hand curled around Kon and clutched his flank tight enough to leave his mark on the taut, muscular flesh there. "Zero. You're missing the point. I'm not worried because we both know this ass is mine no matter what you're spouting off about to salve your wounded ego."

"*My* ego?" Kon's eyes went wide. "You're the cocky bastard. And a greedy one too. Hell, I can see you eying Aven even while you're fucking with my mind, trying to assure me you're faithful. You can treat me like garbage, but you won't do that to her. This time you're wrong. She's plenty enough to tempt me to stray. She's sexy, capable, and loyal, unlike you."

"She's incredible, I agree." Levin's smile was wolfish when he flashed it at her. "And I would love nothing more than to watch you two together while I ride your tight ass. Unless it's fucking her along with you. Would you share your girlfriend with me? Let me take care of you both? I'm not jealous because I *do* love you, Kon. I told you I did. Enough to insist on what's best for you, even if that's not me and certainly not if that is staying by my side only to be slaughtered. I can't have you. But neither can I stand the thought of you withering, alone simply because I can't be with you. I refuse to be that selfish. Because, trust me, standing solo and having no one by your side—or in your bed—fucking blows. There's a good chance I'm not going to make it out of this alive, and I'll be damned if I abandon you without anyone to adore you like I do. It's a nightmare that wakes me up in a cold sweat most nights."

"It does?" Konstantin blinked slowly, then quit resisting.

"My God, you're even more full of yourself than I realized." Aven propped her hands on her hips. As much as she lusted after Kon, she didn't enjoy being an involuntary player in whatever madness Levin was orchestrating.

"I thought you do-gooder types liked when people told the truth?" Levin shot a too-knowing smirk in her direction. "Can't blame me for hoping someday my man will let me have a taste of his woman."

"It'd be better if you'd bury your cock inside me while I was balls deep in her. You could use me to fuck her." Konstantin's eyes sparkled with mischief that made it clear to both Aven and apparently to Levin too that Levin had been—mostly—forgiven.

"Son of a bitch." Levin must have liked the thought of that a little too much. He appeared to forget how angry he was at them for leaving their sanctuary and instead seemed glad they were within arms' reach for approximately seven more minutes.

"I'm going to hell for this, but we're about to make the most of this moment, right now, in case I never get another chance to live out my wildest fantasies," Levin rumbled. "You'll never doubt how much I crave you again."

Aven moaned.

"You like the thought of that, little dove?" Levin increased his grip on her, dragging her closer to him and Konstantin.

"What will you do if I say yes?" Things happened so fast then, she could barely keep up.

Levin shocked her when he released Kon just long enough to wrap his hands around her waist—his fingers nearly meeting in the small of her back—and pluck her from the floor as if she weighed nothing.

She saw where Kon got it from.

Levin lifted her until she was chest-high, at face level for Konstantin, and planted her against the wall as he'd done to Konstantin so recently. He left a gap between them, though, as he barked an order to his most reliable soldier. "Over here. Face her. And pull those pants down so we can see what you do to her perfect pussy. You think it's wet already?"

Konstantin lost any hint of reluctance. It was clear that Levin's commands impacted him. They spurred him past any hesitation or inhibitions so he could take what he desired. He grasped the waistband of her leggings and yanked until they wrapped around her ankles. The soft, stretchy material bound the bottom of her legs together.

Both men breathed deep, the scent of her arousal evidence Levin knew what he was doing. "Put your face in there. Get it filthy. Make her come all over it and I'll take care of you while you do. Hurry."

Konstantin obeyed. He devoured her, lapping every drop of moisture from her flesh. Aven slumped, savoring the workings of his talented tongue. Stunned, it took her several heartbeats before she put her hands on his head and rode his face, unwilling and unable to sit still.

"Hold her there." Levin waited for Konstantin's hands to cup her thighs. "If you let her drop so much as a centimeter, your ass will pay for it."

Kon grunted and clasped her tighter, his fingers pressing along the outsides of her thighs as his thumbs rubbed arcs close to the juncture of her legs. Unexpected rapture debilitated her, rendering her unable to form complex thoughts Instead, she burned her bird's eye view of the men—Kon between her legs and Levin immediately behind him, both of them focused on her slick core—into her memory.

Levin admired the picture they made for a few precious seconds before he adjusted their position, draping her legs over Kon's ripped shoulders.

"You've got her?" Levin crooned into Konstantin's ear before taking the lobe of it between his teeth.

Konstantin nodded, the motion causing Levin to tug on his flesh.

"Good boy." Levin's palms glided down Konstantin's sides before patting his ass. Then he fisted one hand in Konstantin's shaggy hair and used the raw grip to direct his boyfriend's face to Aven's pussy. "Lick it."

Konstantin did. He lapped at her, his tongue swirling around her clit in between passes along her entire slit.

"That's right. Really go at it." Levin waited as Kon did what he was told. Then he yanked his head back, tugging on the strands of hair in his grasp, making both Kon and Aven groan at the loss. "Give me a taste of her."

Aven thought she might come on the spot when Konstantin angled his face toward Levin and let his boyfriend kiss him while his lips were glazed with the arousal they inspired in her. The men consumed each other as if they couldn't get enough of her flavor or sharing it with each other. And when they'd savored every morsel, Levin pushed Konstantin back into her.

"We're running out of time. There's certainly not enough to do this right." Levin swallowed hard.

"Feels perfect to me." She panted, her hand massaging Konstantin's scalp.

He looked up at her, his eyes dilated as if he was drunk on pleasure. Levin chuckled. "That mouth is pretty talented, isn't it?"

Aven slapped her other hand over her mouth to stifle a cry when Konstantin showed her exactly how good he could be.

"Should I reward him for how hard he's about to make you come?" Levin was surely only asking to rile Kon up further, because she was positive he was going to take care of the man between them no matter what she responded.

Aven nodded, afraid to speak in case it came out as a passion-laced scream.

Levin reached around Konstantin's waist and undid his jeans, flicking open the button and unzipping them in a single, practiced motion. Then he crouched and yanked, baring Konstantin to mid-thigh. His cock tumbled out, hard and even more impressive than she'd imagined after their kiss in her bed or her seat on his lap in the hot tub.

"I see you still don't own any underwear." Levin used one hand to stroke Konstantin's erection as the other vanished behind Kon. She assumed Levin was teasing Kon's ass when he jerked and groaned before settling into Levin's grasp. "Naughty boy."

Aven's head tipped back but she refused to let her eyelids sink, determined to catalog every lurid detail of the men's exchange so she could replay it in her mind every time she needed relief for the rest of her life.

"Show her what I'm doing to you," Levin insisted to Kon. "I hate to rush, but we don't have time for me to do things properly."

"Don't want to wait. Go. Just do it." Konstantin shoved his ass backward even as he adjusted his grip on her. Supported by the wall at her back and her knees hooked over his shoulders, she had no doubt she was secure even when he shifted one hand to her ass to brace her while the other probed her entrance.

"Holy shit." It wasn't going to take much to set her off. Not with the air supercharged with their frantic ill-fated desire.

Konstantin began to press inside even as his breath hitched and he hissed.

"We can't do much dry. My pinky with some spit, maybe. I won't tear you." Levin's voice was rife with disappointment. Konstantin's fingers backed away from Aven's pussy.

"She's plenty wet," Konstantin reported to his boyfriend. "No reason for me to stop. Can I keep going, Levin?"

Levin chuckled but stopped her heart when he said, "No."

"What?" she croaked. They wouldn't possibly leave her like this, would they?

"Not yet." Levin rose, sucking on Kon's neck for a moment before turning to her. "Our boy is smart. Soak my fingers. Get them wet enough that I can stretch him. Then give me more so I don't ruin him when I pound his tight ass."

"You always wreck me when you fuck me." Konstantin shivered between them. "But only in the best of ways."

Levin's touch was so different from Kon's. Without tentative probing. No caresses or teasing at her entrance. When he fit his fingers to her, he held her stare then pressed forward, filling her inch by inch with two of them as he stretched her to fit around him. Her body making way for his.

Her toes curled in the supple leather of her aviation boots.

Levin pumped into her, forward and back, until his curled knuckles bumped her core. She hugged him as he withdrew, stroking her insides before he reluctantly departed. His hand glistened in the golden light of the impending sunset, which caused the window to glow.

"That'll do." He spread his fingers, watching as her arousal formed a pearlescent web between them, before returning them to Konstantin's bottom. "Let me in, boy."

Konstantin spread his legs and a calm came over him as he continued to relay Levin's actions to her, mimicking them on her pussy. He slid inside her easily now that Levin had opened her for him with his thicker fingers. Kon didn't seem to have any trouble accepting Levin within him as comfortably as she had.

His soft grunt was accompanied by him rocking backward to meet Levin's invasion even as he dropped his head so he could suck on her clit. He wrapped his lips around it, his tongue pulsing as he drew gently on her, all while matching the beat of his hand in her pussy to Levin's in his ass.

She couldn't see as many details as she would have liked, but when Aven looked down, the position and movement of Levin's left arm made it clear he was jerking

Konstantin off with long, slow strokes in time to the penetrations of Kon's ass and her pussy.

Aven had listened to her friends rave about their sex lives and how sharing ecstasy with more than one person exponentially boosted the pleasure they could give each other, but until that instant, she hadn't realized exactly how overwhelming such a potent blast of rapture could be. She clutched Kon's head and Levin's shoulder, her nails digging into it the way his fingers had to Konstantin's flank earlier.

He met her stare and had the audacity to grin in the middle of the vortex of intense sensation and high emotions swirling around them, making her forget about everything outside the confines of that single homey room. No bad guys existed there. Only pure awe and the natural response of her body—no, her entire being—to the men standing before her, inviting her into this part of their world.

Konstantin took his lips from her, kissing her clit lightly, barely long enough to say, "More."

"Not going to be able to do this right." Levin squeezed his eyes closed, then rubbed the side of his face against Konstantin's.

"Anything is better than nothing. Do it. Fuck me."

Aven arched, her pussy clamping around his hand at the thought of the front row seat she'd have to observe them going at it.

"You're into spying on us?" Levin withdrew his fingers from Konstantin and let go of Kon's cock, leaving it to bob heavy between his thighs, though only long enough for him to rip open his own pants. She craned her neck forward so she could peer down the length of Kon's back, licking her lips subconsciously at the sight of Levin's hard-on. It was darker than Kon's and proportional to his bigger frame. But Konstantin didn't seem intimidated.

"Maybe someday I'll let you taste it, but if you put your mouth on me now I'll explode before I make it inside him." Levin growled as he fisted himself with the hand that had probed Kon, squeezing the base of his erection.

He put his other hand between her legs, near Konstantin's, but this time didn't wait to drill into her, instead sliding in alongside his partner's fingers. The fullness of hosting both men at once expanded more than only her pussy, growing her understanding of the highs sex could reach so that she felt like a virgin all over again, experiencing things she'd never imagined.

Levin made more than one pass this time, transferring her arousal to his shaft, stroking and coating it until he was satisfied it was lubed enough to proceed. He smacked Kon's ass and muttered in his ear, "I've missed you. And your tight ass."

Konstantin stiffened all over, his cock leaking onto the floor as he maintained his rhythm within her despite Levin's advance. She was certain Levin had breached Kon's ass when both men cursed in Russian, their voices harsh and needy if still hushed.

Never once did Konstantin bobble her.

He was a rockstar. Taking and giving like he'd been designed for dirty multitasking.

When Levin's pelvis slapped Kon's ass and he was fully imbedded, he whispered into Kon's ear, "Let me taste your girlfriend, boy."

Konstantin scissored his fingers inside her as if to make up for the loss of his lips when he turned his head. Levin kissed him, spearing his tongue into Konstantin's mouth as if to sop up every bit of her cream. And when she thought his hunger couldn't become any more ravenous, he began to pump into Konstantin from behind while he leaned in and sampled directly from the source.

Was it his teeth inflicting the sharper sensation a moment before his flattened tongue soothed the tiny hurt? She wasn't sure but she wished he'd done it again.

Instead, he retreated, staring straight into her eyes as he began to fuck in earnest.

"No more screwing around, Konstantin. Make her come and I'll flood this ass. Fill it so full that maybe this time you won't forget who it belongs to." Levin's stream of dirty talk turned choppy, divided by the rushes of his breath. His arm worked faster as he pumped Konstantin's cock in time to the powerful thrusts he made between Konstantin's cheeks.

Kon flew into action. His hand gyrated between her legs so that his fingers spiraled within her like one of her favorite vibrators. His tongue fluttered over her clit, alternating with long draws from his lips, ensuring she was about to take off in his arms.

"Yes, like that. She's almost there." Levin shoved Konstantin into her with every rough pass.

Aven locked her gaze on Konstantin's when she came on his face and unraveled around his fingers. She might have blacked out if she hadn't been so focused on witnessing what they did to each other.

"Is she crushing your hand? Good, you can take it. Damn, Kon, look how much she loves that. Her pussy is sucking on your fingers. Don't stop now. Keep going. Draw it out and make it the best she's ever had. In fact, why don't you join her? Come so she knows you loved how her pussy smothered you while I impaled you on my dick."

Konstantin twitched in Levin's hold. He cried out

against Aven's sopping flesh. The reverberations of his stifled shout triggered aftershocks that ran through her muscles like mini lightning bolts.

"Ah, that's it. Good boy. Now squeeze my dick with that ass while I milk you dry." Levin growled against Kon's shoulder and the crook of his neck, pounding into his boyfriend, pumping his cock until Kon's shudders began to subside.

Only then did Levin give Konstantin one last directive. The golden halo around his pupils blazed when he asked for what he craved most. "Kiss me as I fill you up."

Rainbows danced in Aven's vision as the two men met, their lips gentle when nothing else about their liaison had been. She ran her fingers through their hair, petting them both as they indulged in the sweetest kiss she'd ever seen. That was what it took to set Levin off. He unloaded while lodged as far inside Konstantin as he could reach though she suspected it was not nearly as deep as she was sure he would like to be.

Because even his long, thick cock couldn't reach Konstantin's soul.

Kon softened. He accepted every pulse Levin had to give him before he flashed sad eyes to hers. They both knew this interlude had only been a temporary reprieve from their situation, which would have to get worse before it had any chance at getting better.

"Time's up," Sola barked over their comms. "Chatter from Levin's network shows people have realized he isn't in his suite. He has to get back there and introduce the help before someone figures out where he's gone or, worse, suspects something's fishy and makes our agents."

Konstantin lowered Aven gently to the ground, keeping his hands on her hips until she was sure she wouldn't collapse into a puddle of satisfied goo. Then he bent and set her leggings into place, erasing all signs that he'd just given her the best orgasm of her life.

"I'm sorry. Both of you." Levin wiped his hand on the tail of his shirt, then tucked his semi into his pants and zipped them while Kon took care of himself. "This isn't how I would have chosen for this to happen. None of this is. And now I do have to go."

"Take me with you," Kon begged Levin.

"How? Everyone thinks you were taken hostage. And they're aware men like us don't let their enemies live long."

"Tell them you searched for me. That you don't let your men go so easily and that no one takes what's yours." Kon was clearly talking about more than the mafia.

Levin cursed. He spun to look out the window, his hands braced on either side of it. "I can't do that."

"Can't? Or won't?" Konstantin's shoulders slumped.

"Fly safe." Levin peered over his shoulder at her only long enough to make eye contact and nod. Then he hung his head, surveying the empty courtyard below. Snow stirred, blowing across the dead grass into the shadows that heralded the long night ahead. "Take care of each other."

Aven clasped Konstantin's hand in hers. She would do her best.

To her surprise, he laced their fingers despite the devastation clenching his jaw.

"Leave, before you drag her deeper into our mess." Levin didn't always play fair, but Aven figured they shouldn't expect any less from someone in his position, raised to break the rules.

Air whooshed from Konstantin's lungs as he looked

from the man he loved to her and back before slamming his eyes closed for a moment. When he opened them again, their gray was like steel. "I *will* be back for you. You'd better not let anyone touch you until then or I'll never forgive you."

Aven was sure he wasn't talking about sex. Though his possessiveness probably did extend to the physical arena too. Except, for some reason, when it came to her.

It was too much to contemplate while her bones had no more structure than a windsock flapping in a variable breeze yet her mind and heart raced faster than a jet down a runway. She understood how so many of her friends enjoyed—and were maybe even addicted to—their field assignments, even if a large part of her rush was due to ecstasy and not espionage.

Sola, irritated, growled over their comms. "Aven, Konstantin, get your fine asses out here right now or I'm coming in after you."

"You'd be better off forgetting about me." Levin sounded so weary, Aven would have hugged him if she'd had the chance.

"I know. But apparently, I can't." Konstantin didn't say goodbye.

Aven got it. It would have been too final and neither of them could stomach putting even the suggestion of such a thing out into the universe.

So instead, she did the next best thing and banded her arm around Konstantin's waist so they could support each other as they staggered to the car. As soon as Aarav had tucked them into the backseat, Kon gathered her into his lap and cradled her close. She rested her cheek on his shoulder. Though they refused to release each other, they rode in silence.

Aven reviewed their flight plan in her mind during their return trip to the airfield.

And then, she took them home.

Without Levin.

She vowed to herself then, it was the last time she'd leave him behind.

8

"Go, Kon! Kick his ass! You've got this!"

Konstantin grinned when Aven's cheers pierced his concentration. As if there was any chance he was about to lose a thieving challenge. Knox had designed the specialty obstacle course as part of the Shields' training regimen and Jordan had been down with letting Kon compete in the brackets with the rest of the agents.

What else was he going to do to take his mind off Levin, his family situation, and how the urge to taste Aven again strained the limits of his self-control? Though he'd shared her bed for weeks, they'd agreed to limit themselves to cuddles in Levin's absence. He'd spent hours torturing them both with some epic, ongoing edging and gone to sleep frustrated in the best of ways every night.

A distraction was very welcome.

Konstantin had torn through his opponents in the early rounds of the Robbery Race. Now he faced off against Nolan in the finals. A fair match, they'd both made it through the standard doors in the lobby in mere seconds and had been neck and neck as they sprinted to the two blacked-out SUVs parked side-by-side in Shields' garage. But he'd already gained an edge by the time he'd broken in and hotwired his before Nolan had even finished jimmying his open.

Konstantin took off for the gym. Pumping his arms, he tore around the track, relishing the burn in his calves as he scrambled up the rock-climbing wall to one of the two safes perched on the platform at the top.

Glancing over the edge, he caught a glimpse of Nolan's coiffed hair. How did he manage not to get even the slightest bit messed up during the race? Then his forehead came into view as he scaled the wall. Konstantin held his breath, then laid his ear on the metal box.

Laurel and Jace shouted encouragement to their man while Aven and Karolena rooted for Konstantin. The rest of the Shields hooted and whistled for whomever made a worthy move.

Kon twirled the dial on the safe so that the final pin fell neatly into place. He yanked the handle and grabbed the sack of "jewels" inside before rappelling down the side of the climbing wall and bolting for the stairs to the basement. He leaned forward, planted his hands halfway down the railing, then swung his body so that he landed on the floor below, skipping the steps entirely.

"Damn! Nice one!" Tavish clapped for him as Konstantin took a moment to study the crisscrossed field of lasers in front of him. He was grateful for once that he wasn't the largest dude around when he snaked through the red beams of light, contorting himself however needed to thread his way between them without disrupting any.

A buzzer sounded behind him as Nolan clipped one and incurred a five-second penalty, but Kon had already set the sack of loot on the designated plate. Its weight unleashed a moving target at the far end of the shooting range, simulating a shot a burglar might have to take while in a getaway vehicle.

Guns had never been his favorite part of his life of petty crime, but he could shoot. Levin had made sure of that. Konstantin snatched the pistol from the felt-lined shelf and aimed. He exhaled, steadied himself, then hit the bullseye on the first try before engaging the safety and setting the weapon down neatly in place.

"Impressive." Jordan nodded from the sidelines where he stood, arms crossed.

"Thanks." Konstantin panted as he braced his hands on his knees and dragged in a few deep pulls of air. Other than when he'd been coming into Levin's fist while drinking Aven's pleasure, he couldn't remember the last time he'd felt so alive or as proud of himself.

"Good game, man." Nolan approached and shook his hand. "I guess my streak had to come to an end sometime. You know, I'm the only one out of the group who doesn't have a permanent partner..."

"I was thinking the same thing." Jordan cupped his chin with his thumb on one side and his fingers on the other as he looked between the two of them.

The rest of the Shields gathered around them, excitedly rehashing the highlights of the event.

Aven held out her hand, palm up, in front of Marcus, who slapped a hundred-dollar bill into it.

"You bet on me?" Konstantin tipped his head, his chest constricting far more than it had after his sprint. "Even though Levin didn't think I was good enough to keep around?"

"Of course I did. I'm smarter than him." Aven pocketed the cash then hopped, winding her arms loosely about Konstantin's neck and her legs around his waist, planting a loud, smacking kiss on his cheek. It was the best reward he could have asked for, aside from her faith in his abilities. "Besides, it was easy money. I saw you pick that lock at your grandma's house. You're the best thief we've ever had at Shields."

"Winner's circle picture!" James called as he snapped a photo of Aven beaming at Konstantin while hugging him like a koala climbing a tree.

Konstantin didn't give a shit about the stupid grin plastered on his face. It felt so good to be recognized for his talents in a place he was able to be himself. One where the only people who got hurt were those who deserved it.

"The man earned a *real* kiss for that performance, Aven," Cash, Sola's other boyfriend, ribbed them as if they were any other members of the team. Belonging, being accepted for who and what he was, filled a space in Konstantin he hadn't realized was empty.

He laughed along with the Shields until he caught on that Aven hadn't joined in. "What?"

She shifted as if to put her feet back on the ground, but he kept her where she was, right where he liked her, with his hands on her ass and her pliable body pressed tight to him.

Aven refused to look at him when she confessed, "I wish I had the right."

They'd both been exhausted, physically and mentally, when they'd returned from their latest trip to Russia. Though they'd fallen into bed together and held each other as they slept, he'd risen before her to make her breakfast in bed that day and every day since.

They'd spent a ton of time getting to know each other as he'd ridden along with her in the chopper on training missions, hung out with the Shields in their common room, and talked until they drifted off each night, but neither of them had acted on the chemistry that sizzled every time they were in the same room.

Until that moment, when his grandmother's advice echoed in his mind. It was time he took care of himself first. "You do. At least as far as I'm concerned. And Levin didn't seem to mind either."

"Oh, do tell?" James perked up at that, the nosy construction-worker-turned-matchmaker.

"They made the most of those ten minutes together, pretty sure." Sola rolled her eyes. "Either that or they were wrestling a herd of cats in that apartment."

"A lion, more like it," Aarav added.

"You don't have to be a spy to figure that one out. Their hair was wild, their clothes disheveled, their faces flushed, and eyes so heavy they could hardly keep them open. Besides, the car reeked of sex."

"Yeah, it was hot." Aarav smirked at her.

Thinking about that afternoon—both one of the worst and the best he'd ever had—while adrenaline coursed through him from his win ensured Konstantin was more daring than usual. He shifted so he could support Aven with one hand, then used the other to spear his fingers into her long hair at her temple. He drew her face to his.

Aven didn't keep her desire for him a dirty little secret. No, she smiled right before his mouth landed on hers then kissed the shit out of him, her eyes wide open and locked on his, while her friends applauded far louder than they had during the competition.

Konstantin forgot where they were for long enough to suck on her tongue, but the flash of James's camera startled him back to reality before things could spiral out of hand.

"Damn." Aven slid down his entire front as he lowered her to the ground. She kept her palms flat on his chest and leaned her forehead on his chin as if he'd made her as dizzy as she did him.

It was odd. He'd very rarely been attracted to women in his life and had at first assumed his curiosity about her stemmed from Levin's interest, but now he knew he'd been lying to himself. He wanted her, and she seemed to return the sentiment, regardless of whatever their deal was with Levin.

Huh.

"So, uh, not to pry, but does Levin still have his head up his ass?" James asked Kon and Aven.

It was a testament to how dazed she made him that he answered honestly. "Sure does."

Levin had spent the past couple of weeks too busy doing spy shit to so much as say hello in the briefings they had been in together. And when Kon had tried to take advantage of the secure line to reconnect on a personal level for a few minutes after one of the team sessions, Levin had claimed he had another meeting he couldn't miss. With whom? His hand in the bathroom? That dumbass.

"In that case, you're going to need to tell me right now if you have any objections to me sending him these pictures to knock some sense into him." James chortled as he tapped the screen of his phone, attaching them to a text message. "In three...two..."

Konstantin looked at Aven, who merely shrugged. Fuck it. "Go for it."

"Sent." James slipped his phone into the back pocket of his tight jeans and whistled innocently while he strolled away as if his job there had been done.

Konstantin forced himself to forget about Levin and the rest of the things he couldn't change or enjoy in his life. Instead, he focused on the best thing in it right then. He took Aven's hand from his chest, linked their fingers, and drew her knuckles to his lips. He kissed them softly, silently promising them both that he was going to do better than his boyfriend had.

He was going to be honest with her about how she made him feel—as if he'd found a new best friend, one he'd like to fuck—as soon as they were alone.

9

Levin planted his elbows on his desk and dropped his head into his hands. He couldn't remember the last time he'd slept for more than an hour or two before paranoia had him reaching for the gun under his pillow and lurching from bed to check the security camera feeds that were even now playing across his laptop screen.

He flipped open the notebook he kept on him at all times. Fifteen of the eighteen names he'd scrawled in it had been crossed out. High-ranking members of his own organization or their rivals were dwindling—some eliminated, some flipped to informants and removed to Jordan's friend JRad for safe keeping, and some buried beneath a mountain of intel on their crimes so they would never see light outside of prison for the rest of their lives, even if they didn't know it yet.

Those three remaining, though… He tapped his gold pen on the notebook. One of them was on to him. He hadn't been able to figure out which one yet, and continuing to dig for evidence or a chance to take them out got riskier with every passing day and every move that he made to bring them down.

It was a miracle he hadn't already been caught and executed.

His phone buzzed in his pocket. He might have ignored it if it hadn't happened three times in rapid succession. Nothing good ever came of multiple messages in a row. "Shit."

Levin fished the device from the pocket of his dress pants and entered his passcode. When the screen unlocked, he gasped, knocked backward so that his shoulders hit the fancy chair behind him. His legs spread wider automatically as he zoomed in on the picture of Aven in Konstantin's arms, his guy wearing a goofy grin Levin wasn't sure he'd ever seen before as she stared adoringly at him.

Lethargy drained from his soul. Everything he'd been through had been worth it if Konstantin, and Aven, were protected and content. Prized by each other and the support system surrounding them. He stroked his finger along the image before opening the next one.

"Damn," he muttered to himself as he lowered one hand to his stiffening cock and rubbed the ache in his balls.

Each detail, from Kon's hand splayed on Aven's cute ass to the hint of tongue he spied between their parted lips, turned him on more than the last and reminded him of his purpose.

He tapped out a response to James. *Thanks for looking out for them.*

It was only half a second later when the guy responded. *Not jealous?!*

Levin must have been more exhausted than he realized because he didn't even lie. *Just horny.*

James sent a laughing emoji. Then... *They're right here, waiting for you. What's taking so long?*

Levin looked back at the notebook before slamming it shut on his desk. *Job's not done.*

They miss you. Konstantin especially. Push him away hard enough and you might lose him.

Probably for the best. I'm not making friends out here, unlike him.

It's not. Not good for him. Trust me. I love my wife more than I could tell you, but I need my husband too.

So now Levin had to feel guilty about letting Kon down in addition to roping him into this bullshit in the first place? Fucking great. He ran his hands through his hair, wishing it was his boyfriend's instead. *What are you trying to say?*

You've done enough. Stop regretting the past before you miss out on your future. He's not going to put up with believing you don't appreciate him forever. And it pisses Aven off when you hurt him. He needs you. They need you. And you need them more.

What I want doesn't matter. What I need is to stop people's lives from being ruined because of things my father, and now I, have done.

Instead of worrying about slimeballs, how about prioritizing the two people who matter most? At least call them. Ruby set up a private video meeting room for you to use. Here...

James sent through a link.

Levin's fingers hesitated before he could decline to use it like he should have. Reconnecting with them would make it even harder for him to stay and to concentrate on his mission but the truth was, he was losing himself. A reminder of what he was fighting for—witnessing them whole and falling in love with each other, because he recognized that's what was happening—was exactly the motivation he needed to keep going. *Fine. I'll call them in a bit. Do me a favor?*

Oh boy...what?

Pick up a few things for me and deliver them to Kon and Aven? Give them the video link and if they like what they see in the package, they can call me.

I've always thought it would be fun to be a personal shopper. Where am I going? The flower shop? A fancy restaurant? Maybe to the jeweler?

Does Middletown have a toy store? He didn't need to tell James he meant the adult variety.

I was made for this moment!

Levin couldn't believe it but a rusty laugh sprang from his chest imagining James clapping his hands and bouncing in his seat at the opportunity. *Then get to it. Now you've got me riled up. Go before I come to my senses.*

Yes, sir. On my way.

Konstantin reclined sideways on the couch, one leg stretched along its back and the foot on the other planted on the floor so Aven had room to lounge between thighs, resting on his chest as they watched a movie together. She'd been kind enough to turn on Russian subtitles to make it easier for him to follow, but he hadn't paid attention to a single word.

Instead, he'd amused himself by running his fingers through her hair, soaking in her heat and warmth as if she was the world's best weighted blanket. She took away his anxiety and his insecurities with her easy affection, which he hadn't managed to do for her...yet.

He could tell by the way she tensed when they spoke of Levin or the number of times she checked her reflection in the mirror and changed her outfits when getting ready in the morning, that she didn't understand she wasn't caught up in some sort of rivalry for his attention.

Konstantin cleared his throat, wondering if she'd mind if he paused the film so he could tell her all the things he'd always wished Levin would say to him but never had.

Before he could work up the courage, someone knocked on the door. With so many friends around, it wasn't uncommon for them to have company, which had made it harder to find the right time to talk to Aven. He wasn't sure if he was relieved or annoyed by the interruption.

"I'll get it." Aven peeled herself off him. The air seemed frigid without her heat soaking into him. "Oh, James. What's going on?"

"Hey, kids. Can't stay, but you have a package." The mischievous tone of his voice had Konstantin rising to see what it was.

"From who?" Aven accepted a plain brown paper bag from James. He also handed Konstantin a note.

"Levin." James stared up at the sky briefly as if they were dunces. "He said you should check it out then use the link on that paper to video chat him if you feel like it."

Konstantin ignored the rest of the delivery, already heading for Aven's laptop, which she'd left on her bedside table.

"Have fun!" James sing-songed, then saw himself out, shutting the door as Aven joined Konstantin in her room.

"I feel like it's been forever since we talked to him. Are you excited?" She seemed as eager as he was to catch up in private. The dark circles under Levin's eyes had been growing more pronounced every time they caught sight of him onscreen during one of their briefings. Aven scooted onto her bed and patted the spot beside her so Konstantin crawled next to her and opened the computer.

Aven typed in the link for him, but before she hit enter, he took her hand in his. "Yeah, but you should know that I'm equally as thrilled every morning I wake up next to you. Maybe more, because you're not afraid of whatever this is that's happening between us."

"That's not true. I'm terrified." Aven twisted the hem of her sheet around her finger.

"Why?" He reached over and angled her to face him.

"Because you're not mine. You're his. I feel like I'm just borrowing you for a bit." Aven peeked up at him through her thick lashes. "And I'm dumb enough to continue doing it even though I know I'll never be able to keep you."

"I'm not your ex-husband." Konstantin rested his forehead on hers and stared into her eyes, hoping she could see the truth in his. "I would never toss you aside, especially not for a man who only says he loves me but doesn't act like it."

Aven nodded against him then, if hesitantly. Kon would do his best to show her he meant it every day from then on until she believed him.

"I still want to talk to him," Aven whispered. "What if..."

"What?" Kon prodded when she trailed off.

"Is it dumb to wish we could get as lucky as some of the threesomes around here?"

"I hope not, because that's what I want too." Konstantin couldn't believe how easy it was to confess it in the right moment, with the right person.

Aven smiled then, caressing his cheek before she turned back to the laptop. "Let's call him."

The line had only rung once before Levin's haggard face appeared on screen. Thicker scruff than usual couldn't hide how gaunt his cheeks were. Still, he smiled when he saw them tucked together on Aven's bed.

He was as bossy as ever when he rasped, "What took so long? Had to think it over?"

"Uh, no. James only got here a minute ago. We called you right away." Aven looked at Kon, as puzzled as he was.

"Good. I'm glad you like it. Now put it on." Levin unbuttoned his shirt cuffs and rolled them up his forearms, which gave Konstantin an instant boner. He'd be lying if he said he wasn't drawn to Levin's relaxed power or the authority that oozed from him even when he wasn't trying to intimidate anyone.

"Oh! He means whatever is in the bag." Kon laughed as he realized it must be something sexy for Aven to wear for their enjoyment. "He thinks we're going to give him a show."

"You're not?" Levin arched a brow, inspiring Kon to obey even from thousands of miles away.

Aven drew in a sharp breath, then slashed her stare to Konstantin, her eyes wide and...interested. "Are we?"

"Maybe, but I was kind of hoping we could have a conversation. How are you?" Konstantin positioned the laptop for a better view.

When Aven scanned him too, she frowned. "You look like shit."

Levin flashed them a lopsided smile. "Feel like it too. I thought you were going to make it better. Did you two really call me without opening my present first? You need someone to help you follow directions."

Konstantin wasn't about to say so but sometimes he liked to break the rules on purpose and see what Levin would do to him for it. "Come here, and you can do that yourself."

"Not yet." Levin shook his head. He tapped something on the screen and said, "I shouldn't even be doing this, but...I need a break. Let me get rid of these surveillance camera feeds and make you full screen."

Konstantin nodded. It was a start.

"Levin, I've been in the command center during each of the meetings with you and those without. Jordan's contacts are thrilled with what you've done so far. You can already claim immunity for what you know and the men you've...taken care of for them. All you have to do is ask." Aven knew Jordan better than Kon. If she was that confident, he believed her.

"Will you do that, Levin? First thing tomorrow? Aven could be on her way to pull you out. I won't even try to ride along—I'll wait here for you if you'll come." Konstantin suspected the answer before he'd finished asking.

"I can't." Levin rested the crown of his skull back on the gold-painted, ornately carved wood of his mafia throne, his throat flexing as he struggled to get himself under control. "I need to see this through. Make up for what I've done to people like Karolena and to you. Three more, Kon. Three more and I'm done. I swear."

His golden stare flashed through the screen, vibrant and determined.

"You're not going to be satisfied until you get yourself killed as some sort of twisted punishment you think you've earned." Rage and terror bubbled up in Kon. His hand fisted, until Aven covered it with hers, smoothing out his fingers on her thigh.

"I can come up with better ways to torture myself. Do you know how long I've spent staring at these pictures of you two?" Levin held his phone up, showing them the photos James had taken and how fucking hot they looked together. "If my cock gets any harder, it's going to split open."

"Too bad you're not here to sleep with Aven, like I am." Konstantin rubbed it in even if all they'd done was literally sleep. Maybe the promise of having Aven could convince Levin to join them since Kon clearly wasn't enough on his own.

"Don't do that," Aven chided him quietly yet firmly, her hand slipping from his. "Don't pit me against him, or make me some trophy."

"I'm sorry," Konstantin remembered what he'd intended to do that evening. To be honest, and different from the man he'd been doomed to become in the mafia. "I don't mean it, Aven. Yeah, at first, I thought maybe Levin sent me away because of the crush he had on you and I figured it'd be fun to steal his woman away. To gut him like he'd done to me. But only for a minute and because I was fucked up about the whole thing. It's obvious to me now that he's attracted to you for good reason. No matter what happens with him, I intend to have you for myself."

"Fuck yes." Levin groaned as he tipped farther back in his chair so they could see his hand cupping his bulge. "Kon might not plan to take advantage of you, but that's because he's a far better man than me. I want to use the hell out of you. That's why I'm going to need you to open the stuff James brought. Right now. I don't know how much time we have—let's not waste it."

Konstantin thought discussing their relationship was valuable, but a man who didn't believe he was ever going to make it back to them might not. Still, he was desperate to connect with Aven and Levin so he wasn't about to gamble losing the chance to share what he could with them both.

Aven lunged forward and snagged the bag from the end of the bed, removing the largest item from within it. A slow, devious smile spread wide across her face before Konstantin realized what she had in her hands: a black leather harness that held a thick double-sided dildo with an embedded, remote-controlled vibrator.

"You bought her a strap-on?"

"Technically, James did. I told him to expense it." Levin chuckled. "Their accountant is going to love that."

Aven didn't speak, though she turned the contraption until she could work out how it fastened and how she would position it. While she figured it out, Konstantin grabbed the bag, relieved when a mega-sized bottle of lube tumbled out. He had a feeling he was going to need it.

"You are diabolical. You know that, right?" Konstantin huffed and shook his head.

Levin chuckled. "Can't ask a lion to change its spots overnight, can you?"

"Lions don't have spots," he reminded the guy.

"If I was there, I'd warm your ass for how smart your mouth is lately." Levin didn't seem to mind that idea. He draped one thick thigh over the armrest of his chair and rubbed his dick through his pants at the thought.

"You like that?" Aven asked Kon.

Konstantin wondered if it would change her opinion of him if he admitted it. But he was so turned on by the idea, he only shrugged. "Sometimes. Yeah."

"Like right now?" She rotated toward him and shoved so that he fell to his back on her pillows, then climbed over him. Aven planted her palms on his chest and waited to see what he would do.

"Move the laptop onto the table beside the bed and angle it so I can see everything," Levin instructed.

Aven left Kon only long enough to ensure that Levin had the best possible view of them before rejoining him. "Tell me how to make it good for him, Levin."

"Just being with me is enough." Konstantin lifted his hand to wrap around the back of her thigh as she crawled closer.

Levin didn't leave it to chance, though. "Start by stripping. If we had more time, you'd do it for him really slowly, tease him, stroke him, make him beg you to hurry. For now, get him naked. Yourself too."

Aven had already grabbed the hem of her tank and lifted it over her head by the time Konstantin could do the same. He loved that she hadn't felt the need to wear a bra while they were hanging out together, and now her perfect tits were on display, their hard nipples exposed to the cool air that rolled off her gigantic bedroom window and both his and Levin's gazes.

"Isn't she pretty, Kon?" Levin groaned.

"Not much to look at, I know." Aven cupped her chest and pressed her small breasts together as if cleavage was what mattered. "I've always been kind of plain and androgynous. It's why I keep my hair so long. To keep people from assuming I'm a guy, especially when they meet me at work. I know it's weird that I'm not more girly."

"Is that more of the bullshit your ex tried to get you to believe?" Konstantin didn't give a damn if Levin approved or not, he sat up and shoved her hands out of the way, fixing his mouth over one hard tip while his thumb rubbed circles around the other.

"You might have noticed, Aven, that our guy is into men and other people who are masculine of center. Including you. Bold, independent, strong people are sexy. You're incredible. Exactly as you are. And if you shave your fucking head, you'll be hot then too." The distinct sound of a zipper ripping open made Konstantin sure that Levin was also removing his clothes...or at least granting himself access to stroke his cock as they fooled around in his view. "Isn't that right, Kon?"

"Mmm hmm." It was impossible to talk with his mouth full of her, and he wasn't about to stop suckling on her long enough to say more.

"You're still wearing too damn much," Levin growled.

Konstantin shoved down Aven's boxers, slingshotting them across the room and as far from her as possible. She laughed as he tossed her to the bed on her back long enough to get rid of his own jeans, kicking them off his feet where they fell, forgotten, to the floor.

"Better." Levin grunted, drawing Konstantin's attention to the screen where he'd curled his fingers around the cock that Kon knew so well and missed so much.

"Concentrate on her." Levin wasn't having any of it. "Flip onto your stomach so you won't be distracted."

Levin knew damn well that if Konstantin spent too much time watching him masturbate to the sight of them making love, he'd explode long before Aven had taken her fill of him.

"Do you like being in charge of our boy?" Levin asked her.

"Uh huh." She nodded, straddling Konstantin's waist

and rubbing herself across his lower back. Her pussy seared his skin and dampened it as she ground on him.

"You're comfortable being in control. Used to looking out for yourself," Levin praised her. "Do that now. Give him what he needs and take for yourself. Someday, Aven. Someday, I'm going to show you it's okay to be soft. For me. For *us*."

"I'm nowhere near as brave as Kon." Over his shoulder, he saw her shake her head, causing her hair to swish along her back and ass.

"I wouldn't trust just anyone with him." Levin sounded dead serious. "He's the most important thing in my world."

"And you think he needs this?" Her voice wavered a bit, as if she couldn't imagine being able to give him everything he desired.

"I do." Kon reached around and squeezed her thigh, just above her knee.

"When he makes himself vulnerable to you and you reward him for it, he feels safer. Reassured that someone's there to take care of him. And with everything changing so fast right now...yeah, I'm guessing he really does." Levin said what Kon only felt and never could have put into words.

It shocked him that Levin understood him so well without ever being told. More than he would have thought. All this time, he'd assumed Levin was simply being greedy, stealing what he craved instead of giving what he thought Kon required. He'd think more about that sometime later, when half his blood supply hadn't been diverted to his rock-hard cock.

He ground his erection against Aven's bed before getting to his knees, shoving his ass at her while burying his face in her pillows and breathing deep to hold the scent of her in his lungs.

"I don't really know how to do this," Aven told Levin as she held up the strap-on.

"I'll tell you in a second. There should be one more thing in the bag, though." Levin told her to search.

When she found it, she must have known what to do with it. Packaging crinkled as she unwrapped it. The splat of a blob of lube followed.

"What—?" He glanced back in time to see her wielding a modest butt plug, already slick.

"Put it in carefully, but you don't have to go too slow. He can handle that, no problem." Levin's voice was low and gravelly now.

Kon's hands fisted Aven's sheets when the smooth, blunt tip of the implement prodded his hole and began to spread it. He groaned and rocked in reverse, swallowing it until the bulge near its base.

"Go ahead, push it in." Levin coached Aven on how to destroy him in the best of ways. "He can take it. Open up for her, Kon."

Konstantin willed himself to relax and suddenly grew fuller. Aven patted his ass as she nestled the base of the toy in his crack. Then, without being told, she smacked him hard enough to sting.

His cock hung heavy between his thighs, leaking onto her sheets.

"Again," Levin commanded and she spanked Konstantin again.

"I like it when he jiggles." Aven tested a few more swats before her hand caressed the red marks she'd undoubtedly left there.

She trailed her fingers down the seam of his balls and

then stroked his cock from base to tip several times. When he pumped into her fist, Levin objected, "Not too much. Not yet. He's got a job to do."

Konstantin moaned, though he was grateful Levin wouldn't let him get too carried away and leave Aven wanting. She ran her hands up his back instead, caressing every inch of his skin, making him shiver.

"Sit up, Kon. Show her how much you appreciate her taking care of you and help her get ready to ride." Konstantin did as he was told. He turned around and smothered Aven in a bear hug as they knelt, facing each other, on her bed.

He kissed her, drawing sighs and moans from her parted lips, rocking his hips so that she could feel how hard he was for her. The entire time, he clenched the plug in his ass, aware of how much fuller he was about to be.

"That's a good start." Levin practically purred, if anyone could ever accuse a lion of being so tame or content. "Now, lay her down and eat that pussy. Get her wet enough to enjoy her end of the strap on."

That was an assignment Konstantin could excel at. He guided her down to the mattress, then wedged himself between her thighs, spreading them wide to make room for him to devour her. He hadn't had quite as much freedom to move as he would have liked when he'd pinned her to the wall during their whirlwind encounter in Russia, so he used more finesse as he pried her open and slid a finger inside her this time.

He licked a swirl around her clit, closing in on the sensitive spot gradually enough that she rested her hand on his head and tried to force him to hurry.

Levin hummed. "You want that mouth on you, don't

you, Aven? He's so good with his tongue, so eager to eat you."

Konstantin knew Levin was remembering the hundreds of times Kon had been as pushy about swallowing Levin's cock and draining it down his throat. He groaned and compared Aven's taste to his other lover's. She was sweeter. He loved the way she danced against his tongue when he licked her over and over.

"Make her come," Levin commanded. "Hard and fast."

Konstantin sucked on her then, making her shriek. "No, no! Not yet."

Levin laughed. "Don't worry, it's only the first time."

"Oh." Aven quit fighting then, her pussy drawing his fingers in as he pressed them against her. She was so hot and slick already that he easily slipped in as far as he could reach.

"Curl your fingers up, press against the top of her pussy, against her pubic bone." Thank God Levin was there to show him how to do this right, to make it as good for her as possible.

The instant Kon did as he was told, she bucked.

"Follow her. Suck her clit now and you've got her. She's going to lose it all over your face." Levin groaned along with Aven when Kon did precisely that.

Aven moaned and shuddered, her thighs quivering as her pussy smothered him with repeated pulses. He couldn't help but wonder how incredible that would feel if it was his dick inside her instead of in his hand. And then, as suddenly as she'd tensed, she relaxed. All over.

As she floated, seeped in bliss, Levin drove them forward.

"Will it fit, Kon?" he asked. "It's bigger than I'd imagined."

While Aven caught her breath, he retrieved the strap on. The part that would go in her was flared to give her the most control of the dildo on the other end. Not so different from the plug loosening him for her. It was longer and curvier than the device embedded in him at that moment so it would hit her G-spot every time she thrust into his ass. It vibrated, too. He couldn't wait to find out what that would feel like when they were connected by the firm yet giving silicone.

"I think so." She was delicate, certainly more so than Levin though Konstantin was smart enough not to say so out loud. The entrance to her body seemed small and tight.

"Okay, then go ahead. Use the lube if you need it. You can play with her more later. Experiment and tease. But while I'm still here..."

Konstantin appreciated that Levin didn't ruin the mood by drawing too much attention to any of the obligations they had outside of enjoying each other and the limits that placed on their session. He tried to forget about everything beyond the three of them and the intimate moment they'd stolen to share, however unconventionally, right then.

He admired the dips and swells along the entire length of Aven's torso from her hipbones to her waist then over her ribs. She was a masterpiece of gentle curves that culminated in her breasts, now rosier at the tips. He was oddly fascinated by her dainty collarbones and the naturally elegant line of neck, which she didn't often display outside of her private space, opting to wear flannel shirts open over tees and ripped jeans most often. When he lifted his gaze higher, he met her dazed stare, her eyelids drooping beneath the weight of her pleasure.

And they'd barely begun.

Konstantin fit the toy to her and returned the favor she'd paid him earlier, embedding it in her soaked and aching flesh. Her pussy swallowed it, stretching around the biggest parts as he drew on her clit to help ease it in deeper. And when the leather surrounding it rested fully against her, he had to withdraw as it blocked his access to her core.

"There you go. Is it nice and deep?" Levin asked.

Both Kon and Aven confirmed it was with breathy affirmations.

Levin reminded them who was directing their show. "Now fasten the belt around her waist and snug the buckles on the sides. Make sure you don't forget the one that goes between her legs. Tighter, Kon, so she can really fuck you good for me."

He feared he might unload before she had a chance. Levin's dirty talk and the sensual stares Aven sent him as he outfitted her with a long, thick cock made his own dick twitch. He blinked as he took in the image of her reclining against her pillows like a queen to be worshiped, a big fat dildo resting on the hill of her abdomen.

He hadn't been aware this was a major kink of his until she and Levin unlocked it, but he was sure he'd relive the experience in filthy memories for the rest of his life now that they had.

"Aven, you're such a good girl," Levin cooed to her, in a tone Konstantin had never heard from him before and frankly wouldn't have imagined he was capable of producing. He glanced over to see his boyfriend jerking himself as he told them how to please each other. Sure, they could have figured it out on their own, but somehow it was hotter when they let him choreograph their intimacy.

"Kon. Face down, ass up." Levin left no room for argument, not that Kon would have dared. He wouldn't do anything that could make him miss out on being fucked by his girlfriend while their boyfriend rooted for them and their combined pleasure.

Aven tapped the base of the plug in his ass, giving him a taste of how incredible things were about to get as rings of sensation spread outward from it.

"Take that out." Levin grunted. "Don't yank and don't linger on the wide part. You'll make it harder on him if you do. Slow and steady."

Pressure increased, then vanished as she removed it from him, leaving him gaping open and so very ready to be filled.

"Use a lot of lube. More than you think you need." Levin took care of Kon, even from so far away. It confused Konstantin, the actions so at odds with the pain he continued to inflict by holding them at bay.

Aven slathered her toy and his ass with cool gel, working her hand up and down its length to make sure it was properly coated. She tapped it against him, then giggled with a hint of nerves and a sizable helping of giddy excitement. "This is fun."

Konstantin looked backward and groaned at the delight and curiosity in her eyes.

"Isn't it?" Levin agreed. "Now, feed it into him, same as you took the plug out. Be patient but insistent. If there's too much resistance, back up then try again."

Aven paid close attention, doing exactly as she was told. She breached the ring of muscles guarding his ass then penetrated until the fat head of her tool lodged inside him before drilling ever deeper. When he clenched down with a grunt, she pulled out a bit, moaning, then rocked forward once more.

"Does it feel good?" Levin asked.

"Yes!" they both shouted at the same time.

"I know *you* like it, boy." Levin's hand made a wet slapping sound as he rubbed himself to the same beat Aven set in Kon's ass. "I meant Aven. Is the toy working for you too?"

"Yup. Feels...great." She struggled even to say that, so Kon knew it had to be true. She got off on bending him over and banging him for their boyfriend.

He laughed, pure euphoria racing through his veins. Filling him so damn full could do it for her too. It would serve Levin right if she took up all the spaces he'd left empty within Konstantin.

He should have guessed Levin was smarter than that.

"Want to know the best thing about your new friend?" Levin spoke to them both, continuing before they could figure out how to speak again. "I can control it from here."

"Huh?" Konstantin was a tad bit distracted—about ten inches worth—but he figured out what Levin meant soon enough when Aven's cock began to buzz quietly and rapture so sharp it seemed like electricity radiated from the dildo lodged in his ass.

Whatever it did to her must have been equally as shocking. Aven moaned and stuttered, her strokes hitching as she clamped onto his waist to keep from falling off the bed in convulsions.

"There's an app for it on my phone. Who comes up with this stuff? Genius." Levin fiddled with the settings, causing the toy to pulse and vibrate. "I think James deserves a raise, don't you?"

Aven cried out when the pattern shifted, wiggling inside them. At that, she humped him instinctively to satisfy herself. The motion did equally incredible things to Kon so he braced himself against her thrusts, his cock swinging below him with each one.

"There, that's the one." Levin's fist continued to pump in time to Aven's hips. "You're doing such a good job, little dove. Pumping into him over and over like that. I love when you drive each other wild. You're so gorgeous. Both of you."

Aven leaned forward, blanketing Kon. Her nails dug into his shoulders, then scratched his back as she dragged them downward in search of purchase. The minor pinpricks of pain only enhanced Kon's enjoyment, his cock sending a spurt of pre-come onto the bed below him.

"Can you make yourself come like this, Aven?" Levin wondered.

"Yes. Soon." Urgent, she pled with Levin to grant his permission as she moved behind Kon, fucking him better than anyone but Levin ever had before.

"Hang on a little longer." Levin turned the toy up, increasing the range of its movement within them. Echoes of its motion reached Konstantin deep inside. He bit his own arm to keep from crying out when Aven chased the sensation, pounding him hard enough that they sank. She fucked him into the mattress, her strokes grounding his cock against it. "There you go, Aven. Fuck our boy."

Aven did until she stiffened behind Kon, hovering on the brink of orgasm.

"Has she earned it, Kon?" Levin asked.

"Ugh, yeah." He groaned.

"I agree." Levin growled, "Now, Aven. Fly for me."

Her cry told them clearly she was coming even though

Kon couldn't see her face. He only wished she could flood his ass with warmth like Levin did when he unleashed inside him. If he could have gotten his hand around his cock, he could have joined her with one or two well-placed yanks.

The light weight of her collapsing on his back in a puddle of contentment was nearly as satisfying. She moaned, long and loud, then squealed until Levin shut the toy down with a wicked laugh.

"You can take it off now if it's uncomfortable."

Kon tried not to whimper in regret when she withdrew from his body and collapsed into a sweaty, sated mess. The hollowness in her wake lessened when he told himself how fortunate he'd been to have her even for a while. He'd never seen a woman as lovely as her in his entire life.

Kon kissed her sweetly, missing the pressure of her within him. Braced over her on his elbows, he murmured his thanks. "That was incredible."

"It was." Levin groaned, his own hand having paused as well.

Aven finally pried her eyes open, her head tipping as she considered each of them. Her face fell. "But, you didn't... Neither of you."

"You did. Twice. And I enjoyed giving you that very much." Konstantin kissed her again.

Aven drew away then, refusing to look directly at him. She unsnapped the harness and shed it, before reaching for him in a daze and hugging him to her. "I'm sorry. I'm sure I could never replace him."

She glanced over at Levin, splayed before them on the screen as handsome and dangerous as ever.

Konstantin respected her too much to lie. Besides,

there were no walls between them in that moment. Any attempt to deceive her would be obvious. "No one could."

She scrunched her eyes closed until he captured her chin and forced her to stay still. "Aven, I don't want you instead of him. I'm interested in whatever the three of us could become together."

Levin was quiet at that, for once. Konstantin hoped he was really listening.

He rolled to his back and lifted Aven over him, setting her astride his waist so he could keep sipping from her lips as she recovered from her epic orgasm. It shocked him when instead of melting over him, drained and sleepy, she rotated her hips so that his cock nudged her pussy on every pass.

"Again?" Levin sounded as impressed as Konstantin. Good thing there were two of them. Aven was going to need all the dick they could give her and then some.

"Can I have *you* inside me this time?" Aven asked softly as she stared into his eyes.

"As long as you understand I'm not going to last very long," he told her as he looked over at Levin, instinctively asking for permission and more, for the man to supervise since he didn't have much experience in this area. "I've only done this a few times and never after being wound up like that first."

"You'll do just fine." Levin encouraged them to proceed as he stared, captivated. "Take care of each other. Nothing makes me harder than knowing you're so perfect for each other and that no matter what happens, you'll be fine without me."

What? Konstantin would have argued then, but his mind scrambled when Aven lifted up enough to reach below her and aim his cock toward her center. She lowered herself carefully over him, blanking out his ability to form coherent thoughts with the slick glide of her scorching flesh.

"Holy shit." He drew his feet up until his knees were bent and his legs made a seatback for her. She settled into it until her body sheathed his completely, surrounding him in her grasp, and she flexed.

"Sorry, it doesn't vibrate or do twirls." The corner of his mouth kicked up in a smile.

And when she laughed around him, it did strange things to his insides. Ones that made him sure he was falling for more than her body and what it could do to him.

"It works just fine." Aven rocked over him, rubbing her clit on his torso and gripping his shoulders for purchase as she began to ride.

"Brace her, Konstantin. She's getting tired. Help her fuck you so you shoot deep in that pussy. I want to see your balls draw up tight and empty inside her."

Konstantin's eyes flew wide, locked on Aven's.

"Is it enough?" Aven asked as she massaged his cock with her pussy. "Am I?"

"It's everything." Konstantin's jaw clenched as he wrestled with ecstasy, attempting to hold on long enough for her to join him. He met her halfway, his hips thrusting up into her as she slid down him, both of them straining together to share one last final wave of bliss.

As if that reassurance alone was enough to set her over the edge, Aven clamped around him so tight he could barely move. And when she did, she took him with her. They orgasmed together, his cock pulsing as her pussy sucked jet after jet of his come deep within her. He painted her with his release, calling out her name as he did.

Levin banged something, maybe his fist on the arm of his chair or the poor table as he cursed. Not in anger, but out of desire with no outlet. Konstantin would have felt bad for him if it hadn't been his own damn fault. "You two are incredible. Fuck. The hottest thing I've ever seen in my life."

Konstantin jerked beneath Aven, a few final spurts erupting from his body and landing in hers. This time, they both went limp. She splayed over his chest. He hugged her to him, never intending to let go. Maybe, just maybe, he wouldn't have to.

She kissed the crook of his neck, whispering how much he'd pleased her.

Finally, he opened his eyes and saw Levin stroking himself furiously, not even blinking as he stared at them entwined. When he noticed them watching him, he said, "I can see your come leaking out of her, sliding down your balls."

"Sure is." Konstantin didn't have to look. He could feel it, but he didn't give a fuck. He might not care about anything that required him to move from her bed and her arms ever again.

"If you were here, would you be adding to it?" Aven recovered faster than Kon. She started to turn the tables on Levin, dirty talking as his fist flashed over his length, stiffer than Konstantin could ever remember seeing it before.

"I bet you couldn't wait for your turn," Konstantin added. "You'd shove your dick in her right next to mine and fill her up. Her pussy is so soft, and so hot. You wouldn't be able to resist."

Levin groaned, his entire body stiffening, gathering...

Right before Ruby appeared on the screen, a horrified look on her face.

"Rubes! Not now!" Aven shouted, fishing unsuccessfully for the sheets.

"So sorry. But someone's watching. And it's not me. This line has been compromised." The furious clicking of a keyboard that accompanied her curt warning made Kon sure she was trying to figure out who and shut them down even as she spoke. "Get the fuck out of there, Levin."

"Where to?" Konstantin struggled to sit up, clutching Aven to him. "He has nowhere to go. And no one to help."

"I'm sending our backup that way." Ruby spoke rapid fire as Levin leapt to his feet and stuffed his cock in his pants, at least enough to button them around his hips.

His shirt was untucked, his hair disheveled as he ripped open his desk drawer and snatched a gun from within it. He'd already sprung to his feet by the time the door to his office was kicked open. The first two men who piled through it—weapons aimed directly at Levin's head —dropped to the ground, dead before they'd taken so much as two steps over the threshold.

Aven screamed. It sounded like she was at the end of a long tunnel.

Konstantin could only sit there, clutching her, unable to decide if he should close his eyes or keep them open.

Levin took one last peek at the laptop screen and said, "None of this was your fault. I love you. Both of you. You'll be fine without me."

With that, he launched himself over the desk.

Ruby switched the view on their laptop screen to one from a security camera. It gave an alternate view of Levin's office that included the area in front of his own computer, likely so she could direct the support that Kon already knew would be too little too late.

The inevitability of the situation didn't stop Levin. He went wild, taking out pieces of trash that were intent on ending his reign. For as many as he handled, a few dodged his wrath. Despite landing several blows—including one to Levin's temple that spawned a rivulet of blood, which ran down his face—they fell one after another.

It was then Levin paused, obviously focused on something—someone—they couldn't see. But Konstantin heard the disgust in his voice when he spat, "And then there was one."

Levin stood tall, fearless, as he stalked toward the last person on his list still breathing. Unfortunately the rest of his men, who'd obviously figured out he'd turned against them, were closing in.

Even a lion couldn't stand alone against a pack of hyenas.

"I should be there!" Kon wailed against Aven's bare body.

"I'm so glad you're not." She cried, tears streaming down her face as Levin got walloped by a fist to his eye socket, then another to the back of his skull. He staggered, dropping to one knee. When his gun ran out of bullets, he bludgeoned his attackers with it. There were too many of them for any single person to overcome. A well placed kick dropped him. Sickening thuds accompanied the boots he took to the ribs.

Traitors weren't treated kindly in their world.

In fact, Konstantin braced himself for a shot from the new kingpin's gun. He gathered Aven close and buried her face in his neck so she wouldn't be traumatized any worse.

The bang never came.

"Stop. Enough." From his place in the shadowy hallway, beyond the reach of the office security camera, the usurper called off his mob.

Levin sprawled on the floor, unmoving, not even to moan or wipe the blood from his once-handsome face.

"We need him to talk or we'll never figure out who flipped him and why. Don't forget his laptop. The answer probably has something to do with how much he liked watching his soldier take it up the ass. Bring him with us, we'll get it out of him before he begs us to die."

Konstantin had always known this was his fault. And now Levin was going to be tortured and killed.

Because of him.

Everything around him—including Aven shaking him and screaming his name—faded away as he stood, got dressed, and marched down to the Shields' command center.

11

———

"Kon, what are you going to do?" Aven caught up to him and grabbed his hand, but she didn't try to stop him. She held on and matched his pace as he strode to the elevator.

"I'm going to insist that Jordan send me back." And he wouldn't be taking no for an answer.

"Can you help?" Again, she didn't try to convince him to stay and he felt the last piece click into place. As surely as he'd always felt that Levin was his person, he knew that Aven somehow was too. Maybe even more so given the confidence she had in him.

"I think so. I have to try."

"Okay, I'll do my best to back you up with Jordan and fly you there once there's a plan." She peered up at him with worried eyes as they got into the waiting elevator and began to descend.

It was the hottest thing he'd ever seen. That she was so compatible with him in bed and trusted him out of it, made him feel like the superhero he was going to have to become to rescue Levin against all odds. Konstantin took their joined hands and pinned them to the shiny metal wall as he leaned in and kissed her—partly in farewell, just in case, partly as a means to soothe himself after what they'd witnessed, and mostly because he regretted that the aftermath of their profound connection had been ruined.

When the doors opened, they jogged side by side the rest of the way to the command center. It buzzed with agents coming and going, people on the phone, Ruby flinging information onscreen, and the discussion James and Jordan were having where they huddled together at the head of the table, building a mission plan.

The moment they entered, everyone paused.

Ruby said, "I'm so sorry, you two. We've been using that encryption for weeks now and no one had ever so much as poked it before."

"Not your fault." Konstantin didn't intend to waste a second on recriminations or embarrassment, wondering what else the team had seen during that fiasco.

"We've got the field units in motion already," Jordan told him. "The men we embedded are trying to track him down. Ruby's got feelers going out for GPS on the vehicle they stuffed Levin into. We'll find him."

"I know where he is." Konstantin crossed his arms and spread his feet. "I'll tell you if you let me go to him. To get him out and bring him back here."

Jordan pinched the bridge of his nose as if he hated his life at that moment. He opened his mouth to reject Konstantin's offer, but before he could, Kon cut the guy off. "I don't give a single fuck what you promised Levin. You need him to make your case against all these fuckwads we've rounded up over the past several months and the rest my guy identified for your more legitimate partners in the various bureaus they work for."

Ace still had a bad habit of saying what came to mind before he thought better of it. "Plus, who can say what Levin might divulge if he's forced to talk. He knows all about us, Jordan. These bastards are the worst sort. They probably already started torturing him and no one can last very long without breaking or going insane in that sort of pain."

Liam smacked Ace in the gut. He turned to Konstantin and muttered, "Sorry."

"He's not wrong. But I know Levin better than anyone. He'll gladly die before he talks. And that's real bad for your pay day on this op." Kon's stomach lurched at that thought.

"Levin is more important than the truckloads of money," James said softly.

Aven cleared her throat. "Jordan, let me take him. He can speak Russian, he knows a bunch of these assholes and has been in their camps before, they already think he's been fucked over by Levin and might believe he's escaped from being held hostage now that Levin is out of favor. Plus he can pick the lock on any cell they put him in. It only makes sense."

"You want him to go?" James seemed shocked as Jordan mulled it over.

"Absolutely not." She trembled beside him. "I'm terrified of losing them both."

And everything he'd hoped they'd shared started to crumble. How could she doubt him now?

Until she added, "But I think he should do it because he's the best chance Levin has. The only option for salvaging the operation. And because he'll never get over it if he's not given the opportunity to at least try to save his soulmate. You can't deny him that chance, Jordan. Not when you've lived with the same regret and had it nearly rip your life apart."

Reluctantly, he nodded. "Fine. You can take him with the rest of the team for backup."

Konstantin would have kissed Aven again if there'd been a moment to spare.

"Your turn. Where's he at?" Ruby asked Kon.

Hopefully they wouldn't mind his fib. He only sort of knew, but he was certain Ruby could solve the puzzle by the time Aven got him there. "You're going to have to pinpoint the location but he's with one of three dudes and I'm familiar with the headquarters of each of them."

"How do you know that? Have you been holding out on us?" Sola asked. Spies who took people at their word didn't last long. Cynicism ran deep among them. It was a survival skill.

"The names..." Aven murmured.

Konstantin pointed to one of Ruby's screens. "Levin showed us his notebook. Flashed it at the camera for a second earlier. You've got the footage over there. Rewind and zoom in on it."

Aven choked. "Maybe don't put the stuff in between on the big screen."

Despite the seriousness weighing them down, James shook his head. "If I ever get kidnapped by the bad guys, I hope I at least get to *finish* first. Levin's going to make their life hell for that alone."

Someday Konstantin might find Levin's predicament funny, but not that day. Hell, those fuckers had stolen the afterglow of the best orgasm of his life. He owed them for that too. It was easier to focus on dumb shit than the fact that Levin might not still be alive to save by the time they got there.

"Can we go now?" Konstantin turned to Aven.

She nodded. "I'm ready and the flight crew has the airfield staffed twenty-four seven for emergencies like this."

Jordan pointed around the table. "Kennedy, you're going. Levin will need medical support. Marcus and Knox, guard the plane or you'll annoy the fuck out of me worrying about her. Aarav, I want you to cover Konstantin when he's on his way in and out, so Sola, you're up too. Legend and Tavish, you'll round out the team for Karolena. She cares about Levin nearly as much as these two."

"They're just friends. Really good ones." Legend reminded everyone, especially Tavish, so that he didn't screw up again by getting jealous for no good reason.

"Without the sexy times," Ruby added as she scrubbed through the footage with her VR goggles on. She fanned herself. "*Very* sexy. Whew."

"Glad to know my selection was a good pick since I bought one for my wife too." James winked at Aven and Konstantin.

"All of you, get out of here." Jordan pointed to the door, practicing his long-suffering dad tone, which would come in handy for his baby on the way. "We'll have a briefing via satellite as soon as Ruby narrows down where they've taken Levin. In general, hang back in case Konstantin needs you. Whatever you do, don't let them spot you or they could get spooked and eliminate Levin."

The assigned agents rose, dashing for the helipad on the roof.

Jordan stopped Konstantin. "Hey, wait."

"We don't have time." Konstantin looked to Aven as she poked the elevator button at least a dozen times. She wore the serious expression that crossed her face when she was already preparing her flight plan in her mind.

"I've lost my partner before. Johnny will never get to meet Wren's child. It should have been his kid." Jordan rubbed his chest as if it still ached all these years later. "When you get there, you can't think about that possibility or doubt your skills no matter what's been going on between you and Levin and Aven. Clear your head. Do your job. You're damn good at it. I wouldn't have said yes if you weren't."

Konstantin suppressed the urge to hug Jordan then. Instead he blinked rapidly to alleviate the stinging of his eyes. "Thanks."

"Elevator's here!" Marcus bellowed and Kon ran, not from his problems...but toward them.

12

—————

This time, when Konstantin glided toward his country on the Shields' jet, everything looked the same but felt entirely different. The land below no longer seemed familiar or welcoming. It hadn't changed, but he had.

Something had shifted inside him.

His home was with Aven and the rest of the Shields, if they would have him—and, hopefully, Levin too.

That was if they made it out of this alive.

A very big if. One he couldn't contemplate because he didn't know what he would do if it was only him who boarded this jet for the return flight. Or worse, if Aven went home empty handed.

Still, he wasn't nervous, though he should have been. Sometime around the fifth hour he'd spent poring over the maps Ruby had sent them of the mafia stronghold where she'd determined Levin had been imprisoned by Grigoriy Volkov—that power-hungry bastard—resolve had replaced helplessness.

At least Kon was finally in control of his fate. And like Jordan had told him, he was capable of having everything he'd ever dreamed of and more, if only he was bold enough to fight for it.

As soon as the jet stopped, he popped to his feet with everyone else. Ahead of them, actually. They waited for him to lead the way.

Kennedy hung at the rear of the jet with Marcus and Knox since the guys would be staying to watch over the doctor, the plane, and Aven. Legend and Tavish stood in front of them, their weapons hidden in holsters beneath street clothes so they could blend in with normies in the area.

Sola and Aarav lurked directly behind Konstantin, prepared to take a circuitous route to a warehouse in the industrial zone that housed the compound he would infiltrate solo, relying on his wits and charm and unassuming appearance to finagle his way inside.

For once, he figured it wouldn't be a bad thing to be underestimated.

Konstantin could barely stand still long enough for Aven to unlock the jet door and lower it, allowing him to pass. He paused on the first step down, while she followed him onto the tiny platform at the top. She had to be as aware as he was that this could be goodbye. For good.

"Want to know something funny?" Konstantin brushed the hair from her face so he could meet her stare directly.

"Weird timing, but...sure." She didn't seem like she believed she had it in her to find anything amusing right then.

"I was always afraid of flying, until I rode with you."

Konstantin realized he hadn't even remembered to be scared when he put his life in her hands. "Of course I was too poor to afford a ticket anywhere before, but that was fine with me. And now...well, you've spoiled me. I'm only ever going to go where you take me and enjoy the hell out of the ride while we're traveling together."

She smiled softly, understanding that he wasn't only talking about taking trips. "It's certainly more interesting with you around."

"Aven..." He sipped from her lips before cupping her cheeks in his palms. "I love you."

She didn't hesitate even a moment. "I love you too. So please, go get your man and let's get the fuck out of here so I can take you both home and have my way with you in peace, huh?"

Konstantin nodded and hoped he wasn't lying when he told her, "I've got this. I'll bring him back to you. See you soon."

"I'm going to hold you to that." Their hands stayed connected even as he backed down one step and then another, dragging slowly apart until their fingertips were the last bit touching for a heartbeat or three.

Then he was running for the nondescript sedan parked at the edge of the tarmac. He tucked into the driver's side. While he would have liked to pull over by the first fast car he spotted and steal it to replace his ride, he understood what he needed to look like—a pissed off, low level, not-too-bright henchman who'd escaped with the bare minimum and a chip on his shoulder big enough to warrant a shift in his allegiance—when he rolled up to Grigoriy's place.

As he drove away, Konstantin allowed himself a single

look in the rearview mirror. Aven still stood on the top step, her eyes locked on him while her hair whipped around her in the freezing Russian wind. He wished he'd told her how gorgeous she'd be if she opted for an ultra-short pixie cut instead. Encouraged her to stop altering herself for the comfort of others. Promised she'd have his full support and devotion while transforming into the unapologetic badass at her core. After all, she'd inspired him to do the same, embracing the parts of him he'd always been unsure of in the past.

"*I'm* coming back to you," he promised, though he didn't engage the superspy edition of the comm unit Kennedy had implanted undetectably deep in his ear during their flight when he did.

It was only a half hour or so before he arrived at the guard shack in front of the complex where Levin was being held. He imagined the other man somewhere in the bowels of the place, pacing a path in their basement holding tank, making life hell for his captors as he bided his time until Kon could spring him. It was better than picturing him limp and wounded or wondering if he was still alive at all.

Konstantin remembered Jordan's advice and shoved every negative thought from his mind. Only good vibes allowed.

"I think you've got the wrong address." A brute came out and whacked on his window.

Konstantin rolled it down and let them and their security camera get a good long look at his face. "I'm not lost. I'm here to tell your boss who killed Vladimir and that he needs to watch his back."

The man stepped away and had a brief conversation

with someone over his radio before returning. "What do you know about that?"

"I used to be a brigadier for Levin Fedorov. I saw him blow Vladimir's head off, so he gave me to the people who helped him go rogue. He told them to act like they'd taken me hostage, instead of prisoner, so he could blame them and get away with putting himself in charge. I escaped. I want revenge. I can help your boss ID and take out these fakes so he can claim it all for himself. Vladimir's empire and the business that belonged to the others Levin fucked over too. So you going to let me in or not?" It was bold to wander that close to the truth, but his story had to be believable or they'd shoot him instead of inviting him into their inner circle.

The guard glanced toward the security camera a moment before someone inside—maybe Grigoriy himself —triggered the gate to open.

The bait had been taken.

Konstantin submitted the car and his body to an excruciatingly thorough search. Still, they didn't detect the advanced technology of his comms. So he scratched his head to disguise the tap required to turn it on.

"Grigoriy's out on business." A guard escorted Konstantin to a basic but comfortable enough room, one that could easily have been found in an airport hotel. "He'll talk to you in the morning."

In other words, they were going to lock him in for the night. Probably so they could verify his story before exposing Grigoriy to an unknown.

Perfect. Konstantin had no intention of speaking to the fucker. If they left him alone, he could easily slip out of his temporary quarters and snoop around for Levin. They'd be well on their way before the asshole ever realized they were missing or that his story didn't totally check out.

"Great job, Konstantin." Jordan's support startled him at first, seeming more like one of his own thoughts than a broadcasted commentary. Their tech was wild, a whole new level from what Kon'd had access to in the mafia. He was glad that the Shields were no longer his enemies.

Kon didn't dare respond to his new boss, aware that at least at first, there was likely to be someone outside his door listening or maybe even watching his room.

"Hey there," Ruby chirped in his ear. "Do me a favor. Go lie on the bed."

"Don't make me jealous, Rubes," Aven teased. The sound of her voice had him smiling as he leapt onto the mattress, bouncing as he stretched out, legs crossed, arms behind his head as if he didn't have a care in the world.

"Great, now close your eyes and stay still for a few minutes. I'm tapped into their cameras. I'm going to record a loop we can replay to give you cover. If they're not paying close attention, it should at least buy you some time once you need it."

Konstantin had arrived late so he figured no one was going to visit to offer him dinner or check on him until the morning. Add in the video loop and, hopefully, that meant his absence would go undetected.

"In fact, if you want, you can take a nap and I'll wake you up in a couple hours when activity in the bunkhouse dies down enough for you to explore the basement. Kind of like ours, they don't have cameras in theirs, so I can't help as much once you're there." Ruby didn't say what they all had to be thinking about the sorts of things that happened to their *guests* in the off-record space or how some people that entered never left.

It also meant she couldn't give him a status update on Levin's current condition, how badly he'd been tortured, or if he was even still breathing.

Damn it.

Maybe the Shields noticed his expression at that revelation. James took over. "I'm sure he's fine. Probably being such a pain in their asses that they're going to beg you to take him out of there."

Jordan chuckled at that before growing serious again. "Remember, Kon. You have everything you need to succeed, including us for support. Rest so you're sharp, and we'll get this done."

Konstantin never would have believed he could doze off in a strange place, enemies surrounding him, but with the Shields watching over him and the suggestion that doing so could give him an edge in rescuing Levin, he was asleep in minutes.

It could have been an hour or four before Aven called to him, gently rousing him from dreams of being held tight between her and Levin in her comfortable bed at Shields. "Hey, Kon, time to get up."

He reached out to draw her closer to him, but she wasn't there by his side, whispering in his ear. Only cool stiff sheets met his palm, instantly popping him awake.

"I'm broadcasting the loop now. You can stretch, do whatever, they won't see you." Ruby gave him the chance to shake off his sleepiness. And when Konstantin sat up, she began feeding him intel. "These guys are pretty cocky. Between the work Levin did—weakening their rivals— and having trashed the rest of Vladimir's organization, they're not expecting any upsets. There's no alarm or lock on your door. The guy on watch has been asleep in a chair at the far end of the hall for almost an hour and no one else has been around since Grigoriy got in and called it a night with a couple of lady friends a while ago."

"This is your best shot. Feel okay?" Jordan asked.

Konstantin nodded, knowing they could see him even if Grigoriy's team couldn't. He was eager to start so that he could finish, and honestly...he liked sneaking around and stealing things. It was a game he enjoyed winning, so long as it was only evil bastards he played against. Avoiding detection and taking anything he desired, thrilled him. It was as close to having a superpower as he could get. Using it to reclaim Levin felt justified.

He climbed out of bed, touched his toes, then did a few jumping jacks to loosen up and get his blood pumping. Before he could lose his nerve, he approached the door.

"When you leave, turn left." Though it was good to hear Ruby confirm what he remembered from his study session, he realled exactly how to navigate to the basement.

Konstantin pressed on the seams of his jeans, extracting the various tools he'd hidden within them and his shoes. He placed them in his pocket for easy access, then blew a kiss to the air. Aven would know it was for her.

"Aw, we love you too," James joked to lighten the mood, and it worked some.

The sleeping guard didn't budge as Konstantin casually strolled in the opposite direction. He didn't creep or hesitate, because those motions made noises that drew attention. The sound of someone walking around in a facility that housed plenty of men was easily ignored, even at odd hours.

"After you pass two doors on the left, the basement

door is next on your right. I can't hack it for you." Ruby pouted. "It's not electronic. Good old-fashioned steel."

Konstantin didn't mind. He paused in front of it, running his fingers down the solid barrier as if caressing it to make it more receptive to his probing before inserting his tools into the first of two locks. That one was no problem, snicking open on his initial attempt. The second was trickier.

His tools slipped in his sweaty fingers. The fumble allowed one of the pins to drop back into place.

When he sighed, Jordan said, "Take your time. Concentrate."

Konstantin closed his eyes and remembered how grounded he'd been when he and Aven had made love. He borrowed that calm and serenity—the certainty that he'd been made for that moment—before trying again.

The latch released and the door swung outward.

To keep from drawing more attention, Kon slipped through it and closed it almost all the way behind him, leaving it barely cracked to preserve his exit route. Then he snuck down the stairs into an area that had nothing in common with the fancy runners or opulent wallpaper of the showy sections of the housing above.

This was where Grigoriy conducted his dirty business.

Bare bulbs dangled from wires tossed over rafters, allowing darkness to collect with the cobwebs in the corners of the concrete box between rings of flickering yellow light. The walls and a floor stained with things Konstantin refused to think about held all manner of torture devices—a table with rusty chains, sharp metal instruments, and a trough of slimy water. The rank odor of burnt flesh assaulted his nose. Nightmares came alive there, compelling men to talk, even if what they said was complete bullshit to end their agony.

He prayed it wasn't Levin's blood spattered on the cabinets that undoubtedly held even more implements of destruction.

Kon swallowed the bile rising in his throat, then edged toward the perimeter of the space. A row of three cells had been designed to house anyone who required persuading, granting them a clear view of what their future held. Screams would echo endlessly in them, filling those waiting their turn with dread. That alone was probably convincing enough to elicit information most times.

Konstantin prepared himself for the worst as he approached the first cage, but when he peeked inside it was empty. Relief swamped him, until he feared for just a moment that maybe he was too late.

"Your heart rate is through the roof," James cautioned over the comms.

"Settle, Kon." Jordan talked him through it. "Whatever you find, you can handle it. Remember, Levin is tough and he's waiting for you. Keep going."

Konstantin gulped, then approached the second enclosure, again empty.

He couldn't help it. He held his breath as he moved on to the third and there, huddled in the corner, knees to his chest and his face resting on them, was the man he loved most in the world.

"Levin!" Konstantin gasped.

The crisscrossed cuts on his lover's hands and arms still didn't prepare him for what he saw when Levin raised his head. It lolled grotesquely before he could lift it all the way.

"Am I dreaming again or is it really you?" Levin

croaked, his busted lip encrusted with blood below a black eye, nearly swollen shut.

"You found him!" Aven's relieved shout cut off, probably truncated by Ruby to reduce distractions.

Konstantin wished he could share her joy though he was glad she couldn't see what he did. Levin had suffered, and moving him was going to be tough, especially without being spotted.

"I'm here," Konstantin intended to reassure Levin, but he should have realized his presence would bring his man no comfort.

"I told you to stay the hell away from here," Levin snarled.

In one sense, it reassured him that Levin was mostly himself—surly and bossy as ever. But it still rankled that even now he didn't want Kon's help.

"I can leave your dumb ass in this dungeon." As if Konstantin would ever. He cringed as Levin struggled to stand, and couldn't, collapsing onto the cold, hard floor before dragging himself toward the barred entry. His tattered shirt revealed the skin beneath, painted with an array of ugly colors—mostly purples, browns, and reds. Somewhere, he'd lost his shoes and one sock.

"They're not fucking around, Kon." Levin wheezed before coughing then hugging his ribs as he went ashen. "They only kept me alive this long because they think I'll break. If they try to hurt you, I will."

"Then we'll have to keep that from happening, won't we?" Konstantin's hands shook as he worked on the lock. It was harder than the previous two combined. He shut his eyes again, this time to block out the sight of Levin's pain. Relying on feeling alone, he trusted his instincts despite Levin's lack of confidence in his skills.

"Go. *Please*. Get out of here." Levin never begged for anything.

"Fuck you." Konstantin wrestled his rage so that he could concentrate on the resistance and fine touch needed to pick the lock. "Nothing's really changed, has it?"

"Obviously not. I'm still the motherfucker who gets you into shit I shouldn't." Levin groaned.

"Is that really what you're worried about? Or maybe you were hoping for suicide by mafia." Konstantin lashed out while his fingers still tried to solve the problem. "Would that make you feel like you got what you deserved? Are you hoping to be a martyr? Well, sorry about your luck, buddy, but you're going to have to move forward the hard way. Own up to the bad shit you've done, testify against these savages, and learn to forgive yourself after you've recovered back at Shields."

Levin's harsh breathing couldn't conceal his bitter curse. "They could be coming right now."

"So shut up and let me get you out of here faster." Konstantin visualized the Robbery Race and how he'd kicked ass there. He could be a legend in his field, no matter what anyone else—even Levin—thought.

"Yes, ignore him," Jordan told Konstantin. "He's freaking out because he cares so much about you. I'm sure of it, because I pulled the same shit with Johnny. I should have listened to him that night. Don't let Levin repeat my mistake. That's a good way to get someone killed, and I told you that's not happening today."

Konstantin imagined what Aven's greeting would be like when he returned, triumphant, and they could leave their worries behind forever. He harnessed his zen and twisted his wrist at exactly the right moment. The cell door swung open.

He fell to his knees in front of Levin, running his hands gingerly over every bit of the man. He told the Shields, "I'm in. But he's hurt. I have no idea how I'm going to get him out of here."

"I do." Ruby's calm and deliberate instructions gave him something to latch onto. "There's a coal chute for an ancient out-of-service boiler in the southwest corner of the basement. Open it and you two can crawl up to the lawn. From there, you only need to cross about fifty feet of grass to reach the perimeter fence. Aarav's got you covered from the neighbor's roof. Tavish and Legend are waiting in an empty lot on the other side of it with their car."

Could Levin make it up the chute? Should Kon look for another way?

Reality hit him then. Just as he'd been insisting to Levin all along, he couldn't do this alone. None of them could. Konstantin relied on his teammates, trusting they knew what was best.

As soon as he did, his burdens eased. The only thing he had to worry about was taking the next step.

"Levin, please." Konstantin hiked Levin's arm over his shoulder and levered them to a standing position. They swayed but stayed upright. "We can finish fighting about this when we get home."

"Home?" Levin asked, a bit dazed.

"To Shields. And Aven." Konstantin tapped into a well of strength then that he hadn't known he possessed. He bore most of Levin's weight as they trudged toward the boiler.

"How'd you know this was here?" Levin wondered as Kon kicked in the grate on the front with a single stomp. Hopefully no one would come looking for the source of the racket when they were used to people rattling the cell doors and trying futilely to escape.

"Ruby. I've got her in my ear. Now, climb." Konstantin smacked Levin's ass lightly.

"Kon, I can't." Levin tried anyway, using his less screwed arm to grab the ledge overhead and tug. Konstantin shoved from behind, but he couldn't lift Levin high enough to shove him over the edge of the bend to the outside. They both crashed to the ground in a heap, Levin wheezing after the jarring landing. "You go. I'll do my best to follow, but I'm not about to slow you down."

Konstantin didn't even bother to respond. Instead he rushed to the torture chamber and snagged a rope coiled on the wall. He wrapped it beneath Levin's arms and knotted it before scrambling into the chute. He put his feet on either side of the metal box and scurried up it, keeping the line between his teeth. When he wiggled his way to the outlet, he started drawing up the slack. As soon as it became taut, he tugged.

"Do your best, Levin." Konstantin held as much of the bigger man's weight as he could, his shoes slipping on the flat metal surface. "Try again."

"Someone's coming," Levin whisper shouted.

"Then you better get your ass in gear. Just a little more. One more time. You've got it. Don't make me give Aven bad news."

As if that spurred him, Levin growled. He rallied, his thick arm plunking into the horizontal section of the shaft. Konstantin flung himself backward, dragging Levin out of hell even as he scrambled to find purchase with his injured leg.

And that was when the tube flooded with light. "Ah, fuck. He's gone!"

No point in being subtle then. "Almost there, Levin. Now!"

Konstantin yanked and Levin somehow found the strength to fight. To work with Konstantin instead of against him. And suddenly they tumbled into the night, bright stars overhead twinkling as if they were on a romantic camping trip instead of narrowly cheating death. They had started moving, half-crawling, half-crouching, by the time the alarm had sounded.

Aarev updated the team through the comms. "We've got a visual. They're out. Legend, Tavish, they could use an assist."

Within seconds, the two agents scaled the fence and raced toward them. Legend slid along the icy ground, tumbling then popping up on Levin's far side even as Tavish materialized from the gloom to take Konstantin's place. The agents hefted Levin between them, Tavish muttering, "Damn. They weren't easy on you, were they?"

Hope blazed brighter than the stars and the moon together as they trotted as a group toward the waiting getaway car Kon spotted only steps in front of them. They were so close to making it.

"Uh, guys..." Ruby's robotic precision stuttered. A pause stretched as if the command center team was debating what to do with whatever she'd unearthed.

"What?" Legend barked.

"Legend, Tavish, escort Levin to the car," Jordan snapped over the line. "Konstantin, you up for a detour? There's a safe in Grigoriy's office. One of our informants says Grigoriy's been blackmailing a shit ton of players in the organized crime network to get to the next level. Since before our operation began. If you can bring us that evidence, this will all be over. You and Levin will both have guaranteed immunity and there will be a hell of a lot fewer people trying to eliminate you, or threaten your family, since you won't need to testify. Ruby's simulation says you have time—barely—if you go right now. It's up to you."

Kon cut his gaze to Levin, then back to Grigoriy's compound, which was lighting up as news of their prison break spread.

"Konstantin? What the hell are you doing?" Levin glared at him as they grew farther apart.

"Jordan needs him to grab something for us. It's important and could end this for good. For you both." Legend refused to let Levin buck out of his hold as he reached for Konstantin. Given Levin's condition, he had no chance of breaking loose.

Kon peered directly into Levin's eyes, willing him to understand.

To his shock, Levin nodded. "If anyone can do it, he can. He's the best."

Kon's heart nearly exploded, and not from fear or rage. With pure, unadulterated love.

"I'll be right back," he promised Levin.

"You'd better be."

Konstantin pivoted on his heel and sprinted in the direction he'd come from. "Where am I going?"

Ruby rattled off explicit directions, her precision reengaged. "Downspout on the rear corner, forty feet in front of you. Climb it."

When he was halfway to the window above, it shattered. Glass rained around him. "Son of a bitch!"

"Don't worry. That was Aarav opening it for you. It's Grigoriy's office. His door does have a modern lock and

I've jammed it. The safe is on the wall, behind the painting of his father."

Konstantin used his shirt-wrapped-fist to knock jagged shards out of the frame before hoisting himself inside. He landed lightly on his feet before spotting the portrait. Swinging it aside, he laid his ear on the safe door, trying to slow his pounding heart enough to hear the mechanical inner-workings and detect the tiny vibrations that he needed to coax the thing open.

Fortunately it was a common model, which meant he'd practiced on it plenty of times before. That didn't guarantee he could crack it quickly or every time. Usually they'd steal the whole safe and worry about getting into it later.

"I could use an acetylene torch right about now," he grumbled beneath his breath.

"Sorry. I'm good but I'm not *that* good." Ruby chuckled.

"You can do it, Konstantin." Jordan sounded so sure of it. "Even Levin knows it. You heard how proud he is of you."

Kon shook out his hands then started over. No way in hell was he going to let Levin down the one time the man put his faith in Konstantin. He went to that place deep inside him one more time. There, everything was calm and light. It reminded him of the sensation he'd had after his super satisfying orgasm with Levin and Aven. And hoped to have as often as possible if they could ever get it on like normal threeway-loving people sometime soon.

He rotated the dial, finding the first number fairly quickly, then switched direction before locking in the second.

Someone rammed the office door, making the floor shudder, and he had to start again.

He dialed in the first two numbers immediately and hunted for the third. *Snick!*

"Fuck yes. Got it." He nabbed the folder and thumb drives inside, stuffing them into his pants to keep them tight to his body as he scrambled out the window and slid down the spout in a maneuver worthy of Middletown's Heat.

His feet had barely connected with the ground when shouts above signaled Grigoriy's men had breached the office door.

"Aarav, don't let them get any shots off," Jordan barked as the mafia dudes began to curse.

A body tumbled to the frozen landscaping behind Konstantin.

He didn't stay to gawk. He wrapped an arm around his waist to make sure he didn't drop anything, then sprinted for the point where he'd left Levin. Konstantin hopped the fence and crossed to the car, diving into the backseat.

"Go, go, go!" Legend bellowed as he slammed the door and Tavish took off, tires squealing.

"Aarav and Sola, rendezvous at the airfield. Aven, prepare for takeoff in twenty or less." James's instructions layered above cheers from the command room.

Levin slumped against the car door, his breathing labored. "That's my boy."

Konstantin didn't even bother to move off the floorboard of the vehicle as they careened around corners at top speed. Instead he laid his head gingerly in Levin's lap and started to laugh, possibly a bit hysterically. "That was fun."

"How did I not realize how fucking foolish you are?"

Levin didn't seem to mind, his mouth attempting a smile despite being swollen. Levin put his hand in Kon's hair, petting him with gentle strokes of his fingers that made Kon feel prized.

"I have no idea. I mean, I love you, don't I?"

"You say you do." Levin shook his head as if he couldn't understand why.

Flooded with adrenaline and the anticipation of reuniting Aven with their lover, even if he was in rough shape, Kon didn't realize Levin hadn't said I love you back.

There would be plenty of time to wonder why later.

13

———

Aven finished her pre-flight checks and took her place in the cockpit, tapping her toe as she scoured the night for the first hint of headlights spearing through the gloom.

"You're never nervous," Kennedy said quietly from the doorway as she prepared to administer first aid and whatever else Levin might need. "Gonna be okay to fly?"

"Of course." Aven didn't blink for so long she wasn't sure what she was seeing was real until the static in her vision turned into proper twin beams with another set following right behind them. To preserve her night vision, she had to angle her face away from the two cars zipping onto the tarmac, but relief hit her hard as soon as Konstantin and Levin were within reach.

"I'm going to take good care of Levin for you," Kennedy promised. "You get us home so we can smuggle him into Middletown's hospital where Jordan's contacts will let me access any diagnostic capabilities I might need. Sounds like he'll need some x-rays at least."

"Will do." Aven idled the engines and prepped what

she could so they could launch the moment the cabin door closed. It was her hyper-preparedness that saved them, when more bright spots appeared at the fringes of the airfield. Aven slapped her thigh. "No. Shit. Not again."

"What is it?" Jordan asked through her headset.

"More company." Aven positioned her hands on the controls and waited like a sprinter on the starting line for the signal to go. "I'll be glad when we're done with this place. It's far too busy."

"Hustle!" Knox shouted to the teams emerging from their vehicles.

Legend, Tavish, and Konstantin huddled around Levin as they carried him to the jet and got onboard. Sola and Aarav guarded their flanks, running backward as they fired, causing one of the oncoming cars to swerve and crash into the hangar nearby.

They piled into the plane, Aarav taking one final shot before slipping inside. Marcus locked the door and slapped the bulkhead nearest Aven. "Get us out of here!"

Aven threw the jet into motion. It felt like it took forever for it to gain speed, but soon she was able to lift the nimble craft off the ground. They passed closest to the people chasing them then, and the fuckers took aim at them. She veered away as much as she could given the strict limitations of takeoff. Gunfire was loud and close enough to hear even over the roar of the engines at full throttle.

She focused on her gauges and readouts as they climbed steeply, committed to flight. "Ruby, anything look off?"

A pause caused her heart to skip a few beats, then confirmation restarted it. "No. I scrubbed the footage from the camera mounted on the wing in super slo-mo. Best I can tell, those assholes need more practice on the range."

"Thank God." Aven circled, taking them higher, then pointed the jet toward home.

It killed her to have to stay in her seat instead of flinging herself into Konstantin's arms or holding on for both of them while Kennedy worked on Levin. What she was doing was the best way to help, so she concentrated on doing her part.

It was about a half hour later when a stream of Russian curses rumbled from the bedroom at the rear of the aircraft. Then silence.

"Someone tell me what that was about?" Aven couldn't stand not knowing a moment longer.

Konstantin poked his head into the cockpit. "Is it okay if I sit with you for a minute?"

"Of course. Once we're cruising like this, the plane pretty much flies itself."

"Please don't take your hands off those doodads. My fear of flying will come back if I don't know you're in control." He melted into the empty copilot's seat, his head turned with the side of his face resting on the expensive leather so that he could watch her. For a little too long, he didn't say anything. She shifted.

"You're incredible," he breathed.

"You were the star today." Aven beamed, then stole a look at him. His eyelids drooped and he could hardly hold himself upright. "You did it, Kon. Everything we needed and more, you delivered."

"I wish we could celebrate in that nice bed in the back. You know, assuming there wasn't some overgrown, beat-up mafia boss hogging the whole thing."

"*Ex* mafia boss."

Konstantin smiled a bit. "Yeah."

"How is he?" She assumed he would have led with bad news if it was urgent. They still had the chance to stop somewhere in Europe before making the Atlantic crossing if necessary.

"Extremely dehydrated, but his jaw and lips are sore, so Kennedy started an IV. Then I had to help hold him down so she could pop his knee and shoulder back into place. She said she wouldn't be surprised if he has a few cracked ribs, though she didn't hear any wheezing that made her afraid he might have punctured a lung. They also sliced the hell out of his chest, back, and arms. I guess to inflict as much pain as possible while keeping him able to talk. Kennedy sedated him and is stitching up a few of the deeper gashes, but...with some time, and maybe some therapy, he's going to be okay."

Aven didn't realize she was crying until Kon reached over and blotted a tear from her cheek with his sleeve.

"He wouldn't want you to do that," he murmured sleepily as he shifted to be more comfortable, partially angled toward her as he burrowed into the seat.

"Well, he's going to have to learn how to let us love him." Aven tried to ignore the sinking in her stomach when Konstantin didn't respond immediately. "I mean, assuming that's what you want..."

He started to snore softly.

Aven wished she had a blanket to tuck around him, but she wasn't about to risk waking him by asking someone to bring one. Selfishly, she needed him close.

While everyone else onboard rested, Aven thought about how amazing it was to have both Konstantin and Levin onboard for once, with no one left behind.

Hours later, she regretted that fiercely.

The downward spiral she executed over Middletown felt like turning onto the street she lived on after taking a really long road trip. That sense that soon she'd be able to shake out her stiff muscles, kick off her shoes, grab something to eat, and crash into her own bed, which always felt extra comfy after some time away.

But when she reduced their speed and banked, causing Konstantin to stir beside her, her instrument panel resembled a Christmas tree, but with far more red than green lights and a host of alarms to accompany them. *What the fuck?*

"Is it supposed to do that?" Konstantin rubbed his eyes with his knuckles.

She didn't answer him. Instead she radioed the control tower. "Middletown, I need permission for an immediate landing. I've got low pressure in our hydraulic system and the landing gear appears to be jammed."

"One of their bullets got us then?" Konstantin asked, his knuckles white where he gripped the armrests.

"Seems like it." Aven replayed the zillions of hours of training simulations she'd run and every emergency procedure she'd learned and hoped to never need through her mind.

"I'm so sorry, Aven." Ruby came through her headset sounding like she might get sick. "I must have missed it."

"It had to have been a tiny nick, maybe even from debris, one that wasn't letting fluid pass until I tilted just the right way. I don't know. But I'm sure that we've got a problem now and I need to concentrate. Kon, get in the back. Let everyone know what's happening and prepare for a very rough landing. You'll need to secure Levin too."

Konstantin stood and took two steps away before

coming back. He kissed her temple as she coordinated with the tower. "I'm still not afraid."

"Liar." She'd bet he'd left dents in the grips. "But that's okay. I'm scared too."

She held the lives of the two men she loved, and a bunch of their friends, in her hands. Not that she didn't every time she flew but, this had to be the type of stress they endured when in the field. And for the first time, she fully understood the responsibility Levin had borne and why he'd banished Konstantin. If she could have teleported her men to the ground right then, she would have without a second thought, even if it meant she never saw them again.

"If anyone can get us down safe, you can. I believe in you, Aven." Konstantin stayed calm as he entered the cabin and alerted the team to their predicament. The bustle of the agents securing the cabin and themselves, along with Levin, faded into the background.

The control tower walked her through step by step, affirming each of the actions her instincts goaded her to take was valid and not the product of panic as she lined them up for final approach.

"Someone send the Heat." She referred to Middletown's firefighters, who had become friends as well as their neighbors across the street. Of course, the airfield had some of its own emergency services, but Karis and his team were the best.

"They're already halfway there," James promised.

"Good. Hydraulic fluid is extremely flammable and if I'm going to have to put us down with jammed landing gear..."

"It could spark. Right."

"We're all coming," Ruby told her. "We should arrive

ninety seconds before you touch down, except for James. His ugly-ass car is way ahead of us."

"Oh, great. You never show up for my perfect landings, but this one you want to see?" She figured if she was going to go down, she was going to do it with style.

Time vanished as Aven did her best to pay attention only to the reassuring directions from the command tower and not her frantic thoughts that insisted she'd only gotten Konstantin and Levin back long enough to lose them again, at her own hands.

And soon enough, there was no time left to worry, there was only one direction to go.

"Prepare for impact!" she shouted as she set the jet onto the runway as carefully as she could.

A hard bounce then another, but they stayed upright.

The stench of burning rubber seared the inside of her sinuses as they dragged down the strip. The tower radioed for backup. "Middletown Heat, we've got flames on the undercarriage."

At first, it seemed like it might be okay aside from the fire licking at their underbelly, but within seconds the jet swerved right. Aven wrestled with the stick. Between the locked-up wheels and the impaired brakes, she was hanging on by her fingernails.

"We're running out of room, we're not going to slow down in time." Aven steeled herself for a collision, knowing full well that every moment they delayed evacuating from the plane, the blaze ate more and more of it.

"I've got an idea." James must have thought they had more than a few seconds to implement whatever plan he'd cooked up.

She wondered for a moment if her mind was doing

weird shit, like people reported when they saw their life flashing before their eyes while drowning, or maybe she'd already crashed and her brain was addled, because what she saw then made no fucking sense.

Until someone shouted, "James! What the hell are you doing?"

Out of nowhere, his tiny overpowered booger of a car appeared like a green streak on the service road at the end of the runway. Though already racing toward the airfield, he accelerated with every bit of excessive power the Hot Rods had overloaded his engine with, then jerked the wheel. The car went off the road and launched up the embankment. It smashed through the tall security fence before colliding head-on with the Shields' jet.

The plane and car tangled with a boom and the groan of stressed steel as the last remnants of their momentum pushed the vehicles along the pavement, but both stopped mere feet before the jet left the runway where it would have wrecked and taken out cars on the road beyond in a massive fireball when it did.

"Did you fucking see that?" Ace whooped.

"Holy shit. Is James okay?" Liam shouted. Chaos ensued on the radio and in the cockpit.

Especially when tendrils of smoke curled around her ankles. "Everyone out! We're on fire!"

Aven wrenched open the door and dropped the stairs, relieved to see a swarm of firefighters in neon-yellow and black coats poised for action. The Heat! Their chief, Karis, led the charge into the cabin.

"Levin's in the back. He's sedated. Someone needs to get him out!" Aven shouted to the figures that became harder to see through the black fog coalescing into a cloud around them.

"We're on it." Karis dashed to the rear.

Aven stood out of the way as the Shields bailed from the plane. She counted as they went. Legend, Tavish, Kennedy, Marcus, Knox, Sola, Aarav...

Where was Konstantin?

Karis reappeared, lugging Levin in a fireman's hold. He was out of it but called groggily for Kon. Beckett from team Heat followed, one arm on Konstantin's shoulder as he marched him off of the plane. "I'm not leaving without Aven!"

"She's coming too. All of you, out!" Another firefighter —maybe Kampbell—tossed her over his shoulder and bounded down the stairs, delivering her to Konstantin, who toed the perimeter the firefighters had set, his arms up and open.

The firefighters confirmed everyone was accounted for before rushing back to their trucks and picking up their hoses.

The rest of the Shields burst from the hangar in smaller groups as they arrived. They huddled together, surrounding the agents from the jet, as they stared in collective horror at the point where James's car had been engulfed in flames and curtained behind a dense layer of foul smoke. An explosion rocked them backward. Bits of metal peppered the crowd.

The Heat blasted the front of the jet with crisscrossing streams from their monstrous hoses, but the radio was silent.

"Oh no." Nolan wasn't laughing, a first for him.

"James! Can you hear me?" Jordan shouted through the comms. He tried again, "James!"

Every instant seemed to last for an entire year.

Until a breathless reply came back. "This damn multipoint harness Eli insisted on installing knocked the wind out of me. Zero out of five stars. Do not recommend."

Tears of relief and hysterical laughter, poured down their faces as James's car emerged from the apocalyptic landscape as if he'd simply gone for a Sunday drive. He zipped over to them, his windshield wipers casually clearing the deluge of foam and soot away. The custom horn tooted "I'm Too Sexy" before James parked neatly, popping his hazard lights on quite responsibly. From within the pristine vehicle, he flashed them a finger wave, an enormous grin plastered on his face.

"You know how to make a hell of an entrance." Jordan saluted him, then Aven. "Welcome home."

Levin groaned as Karis arranged him on a gurney while Kennedy supervised. Aven and Konstantin held hands as they raced to his side.

Aven leaned over him, stroking the hair from his eyes while trying not to touch the bruised portions of his face. It was worse than she'd realized from Konstantin's description. "We made it, Levin. You're going to be okay, thanks to Kon."

"And you." Konstantin blinked at her as if he couldn't believe she'd kept them from splattering on the pavement. Frankly, she was equally as stunned.

"But I almost got all of us killed." Levin moaned, then promptly lost consciousness.

"Sorry, we've got to go." Kennedy wedged herself between Aven, Kon, and the paramedics, who loaded Levin into an ambulance. "It's possible one of his broken ribs could have punctured a lung or...other stuff. Follow us to the hospital. I'll fill you in as soon as I can."

14

It had been the longest ten days of Konstantin's life. He paced the floor in the Shields' common room. James perched on a stool between his husband and wife, getting opinions from his sister, Laurel, about the finishing touches she was creating for their almost-completed home in the row of Powertools lake houses. They stretched behind the Hot Rods garage and their friend Kayla's naturist resort, which would have its grand opening in the spring.

Jace strummed his blue guitar by the fire, singing quietly to Nolan, who was stretched out beside him. Sola, Aarav, and Cash were curled up in a giant bean bag, watching the show while Ruby destroyed Ace in a videogame on the big screen. Some of the agents were in the gym, as always, while Morgan and Devra gave Karolena a cooking lesson next door.

It should have been a relaxing day. One to enjoy with his new family, Aven and Levin especially.

Except for nearly a week Levin had refused to speak to them—or anyone—unless forced to. Why had Konstantin been stupid enough to think freeing the guy from an enemy prison would have done a damn thing to unlock whatever had been holding Levin back from a meaningful relationship?

Aven snagged his hand when he passed the spot where she was tucked into an oversized armchair. "Why don't you come sit with me?"

She patted the empty place beside her.

Konstantin settled into it, drawing her sideways across his lap and wrapping his arms around her. Not because he thought it would do any good to soothe himself, but because he was afraid she'd misinterpret his anxiety as discontent with her.

Levin's withdrawal had triggered Aven's insecurities as badly as they had Kon's. They were a hot mess.

"Your man's still being an idiot, huh?" Marcus asked.

"Stop. Levin's been through a lot." Kennedy covered Marcus's mouth. He drew a couple of her fingers inside and sucked on the tips, causing Konstantin to shift beneath Aven. He was more on edge than he'd been since his teenaged years, bombarded by unfulfilled fantasies. At Shields he was surrounded by examples of everything he'd ever craved, even if he hadn't been able to articulate his desires before. Worse, though it was within reach, he couldn't quite manage to grasp it.

He and Aven still shared her bed, but it hadn't seemed right to do more than snuggle when Levin had spent the first few days in the hospital, or after when he'd holed himself up in the apartment across the hall as he recovered—or sulked, more like it.

Kennedy came to Levin's defense again, though. "It takes time to heal."

Aven tensed in Konstantin's hold. "I thought you said he's doing well."

"Physically, sure. He's out of bed and stalking around up there." Kennedy checked on him several times a day. She was the only one he'd allowed inside except for Jordan and James a few times when they'd had business questions, or at least disguised their attempts to draw him out as such. "But there are some wounds that don't scab over as fast as cuts and take longer to fade than bruises."

"And sometimes you'll never figure shit out on your own and need someone to force the issue." Nolan looked to Jace, who flashed him a lopsided grin before nodding.

"I agree." Marcus crossed his arms. "When are you two going to stop pussyfooting around?"

"Pussy what?" Ace got distracted from his game long enough that Ruby slaughtered him. "Hey, no fair."

He tackled her to the couch and tickled her until diabolical laughter turned to squeals then a moan as he kissed the hell out of her smile. Fuck, they were torturing Kon with visions of what he wanted most. He gripped Aven tight enough that she squirmed in his hold.

"Seriously." James leveled a stare at them. "He's up there, giving off Beast vibes, locked in his tower. Go, Beau, and seduce your man. Give him a library or a fancy dancing meal, whatever it takes."

Aven snorted at that, but without so much as the hint of a grin. She glanced away, out the window, and the sadness in her eyes broke Konstantin's heart.

James flailed his hands between Konstantin and Aven when she couldn't see as if urging him to do *something*, but he had no idea how to fix things between them. So James continued, "No. No pouting, miss. You need to help. If the two of you teamed up, Levin wouldn't stand a chance."

"Oh yeah? What am I, the teapot?" Aven grumbled. "There were only two people dancing at the end of that movie and a whole bunch of other busybodies cheering them on. I know where I stand. It was never my fairytale."

And that was Kon's breaking point.

No way in hell was he about to let Levin hurt Aven, convincing her she wasn't worthy of her wildest dreams like he'd done to Kon for too long. She would never feel less than because of Levin's stubborn insistence on protecting them at all costs, even from himself. Nope. Not happening.

"You know what? You're right." Konstantin rose, taking Aven with him. He'd never get tired of the way she instinctively clung to him, like she had that first night. And he swore right then to remind her that he was never going to drop her, like everyone in her life had done before.

"Of course he is." Devon stroked James's hair and he automatically leaned into her touch like a plant growing toward the sun.

"He is?" Aven didn't seem convinced.

"Yeah. We're going to go up there and shake some sense into Levin." Konstantin strode for the elevator, carrying Aven with him.

"Good luck!" Laurel called after them.

"What if he doesn't want us?" Aven ducked her head again so Kon couldn't look into her eyes as they rode up to the top floor. "Or he's only interested in you and doesn't know how to say so? I think you should go alone. Drop me off at my apartment. You don't need me to make him jealous anymore. And he doesn't need me to stand in for him now that you're together in the same place again. Go be with him. My parents were right, I make bad decisions when it comes to men. I shouldn't ignore blatant warning signs and pretend that something will work out just because my heart wishes it would."

Instead of turning toward her door, he spun the opposite way, to Levin's. "We don't choose who we're attracted to, but I swear to you that if you're mistaken about Levin, I am too. And either way, I'm going to prove your parents wrong if it takes loving you every day for the rest of my life. So we might as well hash things out so we can get on with whichever path is in front of us."

Konstantin didn't intend to let her go, even for a moment, and risk her slipping away, so he kneed Levin's door three times in rapid succession. When nothing happened fast enough to suit him, he did it again.

"What the hell—" Levin ripped it open. He stood there with no shirt on, a pair of jeans hugging his hips, the button undone and his feet bare as if he couldn't be bothered to put any effort into getting dressed. A trail of dark hair disappeared into the denim V. It was a far cry from his fancy suits, but he still had his gold watch around his wrist. "What do you want?"

As if that glare would deter him.

Konstantin directed his frustration at the person who'd earned it. "You, for some stupid reason."

He didn't hesitate—he pushed forward, using Aven as the world's sexiest battering ram. Despite what she thought, Levin would never wound her on purpose. He retreated out of the way, letting them pass. The door slammed behind them.

The curtains were drawn, blocking out the sun as if Levin didn't believe he deserved the warmth or the light. Konstantin set Aven down gently then yanked them apart until the full wall of windows was exposed. Levin squinted, blinking against the flood of illumination.

Sometimes it was uncomfortable to face the truth. That didn't mean it was bad for you.

"Kon, what are you doing?" Levin growled, as though that would scare him away. It might have once, but no more.

"What my *babushka* told me to do. I'm taking care of myself, and Aven, because she's part of me and always will be." Konstantin claimed her hand and brought it to his mouth, kissing her knuckles as she shifted uncomfortably in Levin's presence.

"That's good." Levin settled some, seeing them together. His shoulders dropped and he ran his hand through his hair. Maybe he would be glad if they hooked up and forgot about him. "But what does that have to do with me?"

"You're fucking with her head." Konstantin advanced a step, and then another, but instead of slapping some sense into his man, he put his arms around him finally, *finally* easing the irrational terror that Levin had been irreparably broken as he held the man for the first time since they'd rescued him and survived the crash. "And mine."

"How? I've been staying away to keep from doing exactly that." Levin stood still for so long Konstantin thought he might not bend, but eventually he relented, his arm coming around Kon and squeezing him to his chest.

"Look at her." Kon didn't have to; he knew what he'd see if he did and it would crush his soul. "She thinks she was only a tool for you to use to get to me. She believes that we don't need her as much as we need each other, and if you don't let me show her otherwise, we're going to lose her. Not only you, but me too, because we were always meant to stand together. Don't do that to me. To us."

To his surprise, Levin didn't argue. When Konstantin glanced up, Levin was staring at Aven standing in the golden light, really looking at her, maybe for the first time. "Son of a bitch."

Levin reached for her and dragged her to his other side, keeping them both in the circle of his arms. Konstantin nuzzled Levin's chest, the light fur there silky against his cheek despite the hard muscles beneath it. "I've missed you so much."

His fingers trailed over the expanse of Levin's back, learning its new topography. The past few months had changed him permanently but taught them lessons they could use now. Without those experiences, they wouldn't have understood enough about each other to hold things together.

"Can you really doubt how much I want you both? How it's killing me to do the right thing for once by leaving you the hell alone? Fuck!" Levin fisted his hand in Aven's hair and tugged until she was forced to meet his gaze.

"What the hell else would she think when you're pushing us away?" Konstantin knew the feeling all too well.

"That I'm not good enough for either of you, never mind both of you. That you can be happy here, surrounded by decent people instead of being dragged into my mess and having to look over your shoulders for the rest of your lives. My enemies aren't ones who will forgive or let what I've done go."

"How much of that last night do you remember?" Aven wondered, finally breaking her silence as she petted Levin's shoulder.

"More than I'd like, but it's generally a blur." Levin backed up, drawing them to his living room. He sat on the couch and pulled them down with him. With his legs splayed, and his arms stretched along the back of the cushions, he looked every bit the kingpin despite his casual clothes and new surroundings. Konstantin and Aven curled up at his sides as if they'd done it a million times before because that's where they fit best.

"Kennedy gave you some strong stuff to help you rest on the flight." Konstantin squeezed his eyes against a flashback to the blood and bruises. He traced the edges of some discoloration on Levin's ribs but was less shocked by and afraid of the faded yellows than the sick crimson they'd been that night.

"I'll never forget how fucking proud I was of both of you, though." Levin hugged them tight enough that Konstantin worried they might injure him. He should have known Levin wasn't that fragile, nor did he mind some pain if it achieved the result he desired. "It was right then that I realized I would never deserve you, either of you on your own and certainly not both together. You should have let me die there. It would only have been right after everything I've done. And then I wouldn't be tempted to fuck up what you two have going on just because I'm a selfish bastard."

Aven cried out, as if the idea of him ceasing to exist shredded her soul. While she processed what he'd confessed and the guilt that had clouded his judgment, Konstantin realized Levin was missing key information. "Would it help if I told you that you don't have to worry about mobsters coming after you? You're out, Levin. All the way. I stole a bunch of files from Grigoriy's office that are worth immunity for us both. We're not even going to be required to testify. There's enough dirt in them that the cops don't need to rely on the accusations of two ex-criminals to make their cases. Plenty of cases. There's no one left who will be able to touch us. Jordan's been negotiating the deals, and pressing for more cash that he insisted should go with them. That's the only reason he hasn't brought them to us to sign yet. I thought you knew!"

"Are you fucking kidding me? I think he tried to talk about it but what he was saying didn't make sense and, honestly, all I could think about was you two. I kicked him out. Told him not to bother me again. I didn't realize..." Levin dropped his head back on the sofa and blew out a ragged breath. His powerful thigh unknotted against Konstantin's knee and his chest puffed up as if he was taking the first full breath he had in a while. Maybe years. "You're incredible, Kon. Fucking genius. I owe you everything."

"You'd already know how awesome he is if you'd been paying attention or quit hiding out in here like the Cowardly Lion." Was Aven starting to believe Kon too, that this was fated? That all they had to do was show Levin how wrong he'd been about what they were capable of handling, which included him—bossy, hard-headed, fierce, demanding, cocky, and all.

"If you really plan to try being a better man, maybe you should start by trusting Aven and me to know what's best for us instead of trying to insulate us in some kind of protective bubble, especially if that means depriving us of what we want most." Konstantin refused to let Levin go back to his old ways.

"And what's that?"

"For some stupid reason, that's you."

"No, it's more than that. The three of us. Together." Aven cupped Konstatin's cheek and swiped the pad of her thumb over his lips.

"In that case, someone better get over here and suck my dick." Levin speared the fingers of his left hand into Konstantin's hair and wound Aven's around his right wrist, then pressed them toward his crotch.

Konstantin exchanged stares with Aven as both of them grinned.

"Better yet, both of you do it." If Levin thought he was going to scare them away with his demands, he still had a lot to learn about them.

Together, Konstantin and Aven pounced. They partnered to unzip Levin's jeans and take out his stiffening cock.

15

———

week of rest hadn't rejuvenated Levin as much as five minutes with Konstantin and Aven. If lusting after them both made him a bad man, there was no way he was ever going to manage to be anything else. They were the one vice he'd never be able to quit.

He'd tried, and it was no use.

Konstantin was right. Somehow, he'd found not only one but two people who were strong, far better than he deserved, and willing to put up with his shit. "I can't believe I finally have you both within reach. Fuck, the things I've dreamed of doing to you should be illegal."

"It's probably a good thing you're retiring from being a mafia spy, because we've been right across the hall for more than a week," Aven sassed him. "Didn't think we were that hard to find. All you had to do was cross the five feet and come get us. Or, you know, invite us in. Was that too hard for a big, scary kingpin like you?"

"Just for that, Kon gets to make me stiff. He'll show you exactly how hard I can get. Keep it up and I'll let him have all the fun." Levin shifted, thrusting his pelvis in Kon's direction. Of course, he knew that sucking cock would get Konstantin equally as hard so he could help take better care of Aven. "You can practice on my finger for next time. Show me how you'd worship my cock and maybe you'll earn the privilege."

Levin slid his hand from her hair, using his middle finger to trace from the tip of her nose down to the divot in her upper lip before pressing it into her mouth, forcing her to open for him. When her sharp little teeth raked his knuckles, he smirked. "I'm warning you, Aven. You're only turning me on more. The hornier you make me, the less careful I'm going to be with you. I'm not a gentle lover like our boy and you're encouraging me not to take it easy on you."

She didn't flinch as he put his finger fully in her mouth, instead staring directly at him as she bit down to hold him there before beginning to suck on it. Fuck, his dick was jealous of the things her mouth was capable of doing.

Konstantin waited patiently for a signal to claim his reward, his face resting on Levin's thigh, mere inches from where they both needed him to be. He breathed deep yet fast, as if he was savoring the scent of Levin's dampening skin and balls, only inches from the man's nose.

Aven's eyes drifted to their boyfriend, smiling around Levin's finger when she noticed the near trance he'd gone into, anticipating what was to come and the pleasure he knew Levin would deliver. Levin might have fucked up a lot of things in his life, but this wasn't one of them.

In bed, he'd never let anyone down. Especially not Kon. And he didn't intend to start with Aven.

"He's so beautiful, isn't he?" Levin asked Aven. "Has he been good while I was away?"

She hummed, tickling the underside of his finger with her assent.

"Okay then. You can have my dick, Kon. Go ahead, get it extra hard so I can fuck you both."

Konstantin's pupils dilated as he opened his mouth wide, practically inhaling Levin's semi. The intense and slick velvet of his mouth and tongue were so familiar yet novel again, that Levin couldn't watch. He stared up at the ceiling to keep from losing control and fucking Kon's face for the three seconds it would take him to come if he hadn't had much better things in store for his pets.

Aven had the balls to cackle at him. To actually fucking laugh around his finger embedded in her mouth when she watched what a single contact with Kon had the power to do to him.

"You let her get away with too much, Konstantin." Levin growled, though he loved her spirit. "You've spoiled your girlfriend. We're going to have to teach her how serious I am about sex."

Konstantin groaned around Levin's cock, speeding along the process of growing his hard-on. Aven arched a brow at him as if to ask how.

"Oh, I'm about to show you, little dove. Just remember, you're begging for these lessons."

It was relief, not fear, in her pretty eyes as she sucked his finger harder.

"Lift up, Kon." When their partner cried out at the directive, Levin reassured him by massaging his scalp. "Just for a second."

Kon let Levin's dick slip from his lips with a wet pop. Levin patted his cheek lovingly, then told him, "Get her naked, show me her tits and that pretty pussy. Then help her stretch out across my lap. You're going to use your torso to hold her in place and suck me off while I show her why you love to be spanked so much."

Konstantin nodded eagerly.

"You are?" Aven asked warily when he took his hand from her mouth.

"I am. And I'm going to make you appreciate it, too." He cupped her cheek in his hand, forcing her to look at him. "This isn't a game, Aven. This is who I am. You've shown me you're plenty capable of handling it, now trust me to give you everything you need."

She only hesitated a fraction of a second before rising from the couch gracefully and angling toward Konstantin. As soon as she did, he shoved her tunic shirt up her torso and gripped the wide waistband of her leggings as if he intended to rip them off of her.

"No, boy." Levin shook his head, tsking.

Kon froze.

"Slow. Show her off to me inch by inch now that I can get a better look at her." Levin shifted, moving his ass forward on the couch. He draped one arm over its back as casually as he could, pushed his jeans down to expose his balls, then spread his legs even wider to give them better access before fisting his cock. Most people would say it was hard, but he knew he could pump more stiffness into it, making sure he gave both his lovers every bit of what he had.

Konstantin didn't disappoint. He started with Aven's soft belly, kissing beside her navel then lower as he worked her leggings down. She petted Konstantin, running her fingers through his hair as he unwrapped her like the present she was for Levin.

"You're giving your girl to me, aren't you?" Levin began to stroke himself, drawing Aven's attention to how hard the sight of them together got him.

Konstantin nodded, his lips dragging over her mound as he peeled her bottoms off.

"I swear I'll take good care of her, Kon."

Levin was caught off guard when Kon replied in Russian, "If you don't, I'll kick your ass."

It was a reminder that although Kon knelt for him, he did it by choice. And Aven was the one thing he wouldn't let Levin ruin for the privilege.

It took damn near ten minutes, but by the time Aven stood naked in front of them, she was squirming, needy, exactly as he wanted her to be when Konstantin draped her over his lap.

Levin was careful not to let him speed up. Not that he didn't enjoy the idea of coming all over them both, he just didn't intend to do it so soon.

The tips of Aven's breasts were rosy against her creamy skin, like her flushed cheeks. The long curtain of her hair brushed the top swell of her ass, making his hand tingle in anticipation.

"Bring her to me." Levin slapped his hard-on against his belly, trapping it there as Konstantin laid Aven across his lap, face down. He shifted her position to ensure there was enough room for what he had planned. "For every three strokes she takes, you can suck my cock for thirty seconds. While you do, I'm going to feed her hungry pussy my fingers."

He figured he could last all night if he didn't let Kon work on him too long. But Aven, well, she wasn't getting up until she'd unraveled around his hand, her ass on fire.

She would learn to love him breaking her down.

Showing her that no matter what she'd come to believe, she didn't need to be tough all the time, and never around him. Even if he had to use her bond with Konstantin to prove it to her.

"What do you think, Aven? Can you let Konstantin have his treat?" Levin rubbed her ass, accustoming her to his touch.

"Please, Aven." Konstantin kissed her hip. "Just a little?"

She crossed her arms on the couch and laid her face on them as if she could nap while they amused themselves. She had a lot to learn, mostly about herself. But Levin already knew what she needed, even if she didn't. She shrugged. "Sure, why not?"

Levin shot Konstantin a wicked grin. Kon groaned.

Levin lowered his arm across her lower back, pinning her in place, then told Kon, "Grab her legs. She's going to kick."

"Doubt it." She still had no idea.

The crack that echoed in the room when his palm met her flesh for the first time startled all of them, but only because it felt so good.

Aven arched, but between him and Kon, she couldn't escape. Levin spanked her again and again, before easing up on the pressure. Her legs went limp, trembling. A laugh rumbled through Levin's chest. "You were meant for us."

He drew the outline of his palm print on her ass, soothing the sting before focusing on Konstantin. "Get my fingers wet."

Kon slurped his left index and middle fingers into his mouth, licking and giving them sloppy sucks so they were drenched. Levin petted Aven's shuddering back as she recovered. He wedged his hand between her thighs, probed until he aligned two fingers with her entrance, then shoved, embedding himself within her in a single unrelenting stroke.

"Oh fuck." Aven hugged him tight, illustrating how good she would feel when she smothered his dick.

Levin began to move them in a circle, pressing on her from all sides like the toy she'd worn for him had done. As if the motion reminded her of that magical moment, her hips began to grind on his thigh.

"Clock is ticking, Kon." Levin stole the man's attention from the spectacle Aven was making. "Come and get your reward."

He didn't mind when Konstantin forsook a few of his precious seconds to place tender kisses on Aven's ass before sealing his mouth over Levin's cock.

"Fuck, that's good." Levin loved having his hand in Aven's pussy and his dick in Kon's mouth. It was like he formed a conduit between them, taking her pleasure and feeding it to the man between his knees. But thirty seconds went fast, and soon he was withdrawing.

Without having to be told, Kon lifted off Levin, licking his lips as he stared adoringly upward, waiting for further direction. "Good boy."

Aven sighed, her ass lifting as if begging for more.

"You're not done?" Levin checked.

"Not even close." She shook her head, waving her mane against her back.

They made it through ten or maybe twenty rounds—he lost track—before he understood that Aven wasn't going to be as easy to crack as he'd expected. The next time he went to spank her, his hand stinging, he ramped things up. "Give me your wrists."

At least she'd stopped talking back. Aven immediately placed them behind her. Levin gathered them into one hand, pinning them in the small of her back, and that made all the difference. She squirmed, writhing in his lap before he'd so much as drawn his other hand back.

"She likes that," Kon muttered reverently, watching up close as her pussy squeezed, empty, begging for something to hold. Something he would give her soon.

"Seems like your girlfriend enjoys being restrained as much as you do." Levin grunted and rubbed his dripping cock on her hip. "Maybe someday I'll tie you together, spread wide, and take turns fucking a different hole with every stroke."

He had to be careful or he would lose control, the fantasy he designed for his lovers checking all his own boxes, and he refused to let them down. Not when they'd waited so long to finally be together.

Aven cried out then and broke. "Please, Levin. Give me more. I need it."

"I know you do, little dove." He didn't make her wait, bringing his hand down hard three times in rapid succession.

If she wasn't already orgasming by the time he got his fingers in her, she certainly was before he'd finished impaling her on them. "Last taste, Kon. She's crushing my fingers. Listen to her come while you suck me."

Konstantin's pulls were short and choppy, nearly frenzied as he blew Levin, bringing him to the edge. Especially since he gave Aven extra so she could finish climaxing around him.

"Enough," Levin told Konstantin as he yanked his hand from the temptation of Aven's steaming pussy.

"Not nearly," she moaned.

"You're going to have more than you can handle before we're done with you," Levin promised. He scooped his arms beneath her and stood, turning her over as he held her out to Konstantin. "Have her?"

"I would never drop her." He cradled Aven to his chest, rocking her as she recovered from her orgasm, murmuring to her the whole time Levin wrestled with his jeans, ridding himself of them. "You're perfect, Aven. So strong, so responsive. I love seeing what he can do to you, and knowing that it feels as good as when he does it to me too."

"Being with you is incredible." She licked Kon's neck. "This is too. They're different. And I think I need them both. I just didn't realize..."

The wonder in her tone and the daze she still swam in made Levin sure. "Of course you do. We're going to take care of you, little dove. All you have to do is let us."

"Kon, come." Levin strode—naked except for his watch, which he couldn't be bothered to remove—to his bedroom. The one with the pillows that smelled like Konstantin's shampoo.

Now it would smell like lust and love and...forever.

After he'd finished claiming them, Levin would never be able to let them go again. He hoped they knew what they'd asked of him.

Kon followed on his heels, carrying Aven so that they could lay her on the altar of his bed and worship her together. When Konstantin looked up at him for direction, Levin told him, "You're in charge of spoiling her. I will break her down, you will build her back up."

Kon's eyes were bright as he nodded.

"Can you be trusted with your clothes off? No

accidents?" Levin asked, aware of how easily Aven could make them both lose it.

"Yes. I promise I'll be good. Just let me hold her skin to skin," Konstantin pleaded.

Levin groaned and captured Kon's mouth in a rough kiss, their tongues parrying with each other as he squeezed Konstantin's ass. When he looked over Kon's shoulder and saw Aven playing with her pussy as she watched them, he groaned and separated them.

"Your girlfriend is a lot to handle." Levin jerked his chin so Kon could see what they did to her.

"You can do it." Konstantin bit Levin's pec, his teeth gripping the nipple.

"We can." Levin stripped Kon's shirt over his head with a single yank, then glared at his pants. "Get rid of those. Now."

When he did, his cock sprang out, harder than Levin had ever seen it before. He could relate. Levin told Kon, "Lie on the bed on your back, ass at the side. You're going to hold her while I take the edge off."

Konstantin nodded and got into position. Levin plucked Aven from the bed. He put her feet on the floor so she stood between Kon's legs. He planted one hand on her hip and the other on her shoulder, bending her over. Her torso connected with Kon's from pelvises up.

"Hello," he cooed to her before kissing her with a movement that was both sweet and passionate while Levin ran his hands down the expanse of her back and over her red ass. It wasn't long before she was rocking toward him.

"You want more? You're sure?" Levin goaded her though he knew they were nowhere near done. He just wanted to hear her admit it after denying to herself that she needed someone, anyone, for so long.

"Mmm, yes." She moaned into Kon's mouth.

Levin dragged two fingers down her spine. "Remember this moment, Aven. The last one before you ever had my cock in you. The instant before everything changed. Because once I claim this pussy, it will be mine forever.

"Why are you doing this to me?" Aven resisted. "Can't you just fuck me?"

"It was never going to be as simple as that," Levin rasped against her temple. "I don't only want your body. I want everything—your heart and soul, your nightmares, and the dreams I'm going to make come true. I'm going to expose every fear you've ever had—especially about men —so that I can repair the damage that was done to you. It might hurt some, but it's going to feel so much better when I'm finished."

He pressed his thighs to the backs of hers and her burning ass, to remind her of how hard it had made her come.

"What would you know about my past?" She shifted away from him as if afraid it could change his mind.

She might not have told him, but that didn't mean he didn't know.

"You're screaming for me to break you, little dove. Have been since the moment we met. Daring me and every other person you come across to let you down like others have. You won't be happy until you find someone you can bend around. Someone who doesn't need you to be tough or self-reliant every moment of the day. Think I haven't scoured your history? Stalked you from the other side of the globe? Been obsessed since I walked into this place and locked eyes with the most gorgeous woman I've ever seen? That six-month marriage on your record and the fact that your address never lined up with your parents' again despite the fact that you were still practically a child told me a lot. You've never had a dating profile on any app and aced every single exam in your flight school records—yeah, I can tell a lot from that. And I saw for myself how you got off on topping Konstantin, when you thought you had all the power. I see you, Aven, and I have what you need."

"I take back what I said about the spy stuff," Aven grumbled, making him grin.

"What I'm telling you, precious," Levin wrapped his hand not-so-gently around her throat, his thumb rubbing below her ear, "is that you might be a lioness when it comes to everyone else in the world, but here—with Kon and me—you can be a marshmallow. Remember, he's here to look after you while I have my fun."

"Who's going to take care of Kon?" she asked.

"Levin does that just fine," Konstantin promised her.

"You can help me." Levin gathered her hair into a single rope, twisting it around his wrist, loving the feel of the silky strands binding them together. "Would you like that?"

She nodded, sipping from Konstantin's lips.

"I'll let you two cuddle as often as you like," Levin promised. "I fucking loved thinking about the two of you tangled together, safe and warm every night."

"But now you'll be with us, right?" Levin detected the hint of uncertainty in Aven's question, like she was hoping but not quite sure she believed it.

"I told you. Once I get in this pussy, and then your ass, I'm never going to be able to walk away," he swore to them. "Hell, even now...I obviously can't say no, even if I should."

"Don't you dare." Konstantin shook his head and Aven clutched him. He realized that Aven had done for Kon what he was going to do for her. Repaired the damage he'd unwittingly caused.

"I'm sorry, Kon." Levin met his boyfriend's stare. "I'll do better. *Be* better. For you both."

Konstantin squeezed his eyes closed for a moment and when he opened them, he was staring straight into Aven's gaze.

"I'll jump if you will," she told him.

He clasped her face between his hands and kissed the shit out of her.

Levin had his answer. There was no going back. Not for any of them.

"Kon, change of plans. Move up some so she has something to do with that pretty mouth while I taste her. I've been dying for more of her since that damn quickie against the wall."

Konstantin groaned and did as he was told.

Levin crouched behind Aven, spreading her pussy and ass. He didn't play around, didn't tease. He went right to sucking her clit as his lips and nose bumped her slit, pausing only to say, "Put his dick in your mouth, but you'd better come before he does if you want to be allowed to play with it next time."

Konstantin let his head drop against the mattress. "Oh shit. Aven, that feels so fucking good. I'll try to hold on, but I don't know how long I can last."

Aven wasn't at risk of losing her privileges. A flood of desire coated his tongue.

Levin chuckled against her flesh, then returned his

fingers to her pussy, filling it up. It went on long enough that Kon reverted to Russian, mostly for curses, his heels drumming the floor on either side of Levin. But when Levin thought the boy might slip up, he reached beneath Aven to squeeze Kon's balls, backing him away from the ledge.

Levin pressed down with his fingers, massaging the patch near Aven's pubic bone, making her shatter again. And when she did, he sprang into action. He flipped her so she lay on her back, side-by-side with Konstantin. Their hands connected and linked automatically, finding each other even during the storm of her pleasure.

Despite her quivering insides, she spread her legs for him.

"Don't rush me." He slapped the inside of her thigh, making her groan, and not in pain. "No more quickies. I'm going to take my damn time and you two are going to lie there and enjoy it."

Levin cracked his knuckles as he stared down at them. Konstantin's dick strained against his abdomen, but he'd retreated from the brink of orgasm. He was grinning up at Levin as if to tempt him into the easy way out. Absolutely not.

"If I can't keep you out of danger the ways I tried before, then you're going to help me do this right. I'm going to need backup to last all night." He raised a brow at Konstantin, who nodded.

"Like the whole entire night?" She seemed to think he was joking.

"When's the last time you saw the sun come up?" Levin asked her, dead serious.

"A lot of times when I'm flying. It's my favorite time of day." She sighed. "Everyone else is quiet and I can enjoy the peace and colors while completely in control of my fate. All of my problems seem small, and far away when I'm up there. I guess it's the one time I have the world to myself."

"Your world includes us now," Konstantin told her, kissing her forehead. "We'll be there to watch the sun come up with you for the rest of our lives."

Levin couldn't resist the sight of them together. It was going to become a permanent weakness.

"Are you ready for me?" he asked Aven.

She glanced first at Kon, who rubbed their noses together then murmured, "Remember, I've got you."

Then back to Levin. "Yes."

He shoved her far enough onto the mammoth bed that she rested in the center with plenty of room for Konstantin to stretch out along her length. He took Kon's hand and pressed it to Aven's mound. "Make it as good for her as possible."

Konstantin didn't hesitate. He took up where Levin had left off, rubbing her pussy even as he dipped his head to flick the tip of his tongue over her nipple. Aven stared at the places they touched. Levin couldn't wait until it was his dick she was obsessed with as he finally joined them together.

"Eyes on me, little dove." He grabbed hold of her legs, just above her knees, lifting and spreading them to make room for his hips. When his cock hung near her opening he turned to Kon. "Put me inside your girlfriend. Feed my cock to her hungry pussy and watch how well she takes me."

Kon cursed in Russian. "You're diabolical."

"I used to be. Until I met you." Levin went where Kon led him, letting the other man set the blunt head of his cock against the wet heat of Aven's body. He didn't insult her by pretending she might crumble. Instead, he sank into her in one continuous stroke, stopping only when her body needed space to adjust.

It was heaven, sliding into her inch by inch, claiming her and sharing her with Kon at the same time. His balls drew tight, eager to flood her pussy before he'd even finished fusing their bodies.

"Levin!" she cried out as she grasped his shoulders and hung on, trusting that he would be there to see her through whatever nights might come their way. "It feels...amazing."

"He's thick, isn't he?" Konstantin hummed as he drew circles around her clit, making sure her pleasure eclipsed any pain. "Hug him, let him feel what he does to you."

Aven couldn't speak after that. Her eyelids fluttered closed and she bit her lip, concentrating only on absorbing everything he gave her. Levin anchored her in place with his hands wrapped around her waist and began to fuck.

Every thrust within her lit up nerves all along his shaft and down to his balls, compelling him to do it again—faster, harder, and deeper on each return. He glanced down at Konstantin, who was whispering encouragement in her ear in between kisses and even a nip on her bottom lip.

Konstantin shot him a sultry look and urged him on. "She's fine. You're not hurting her. Give her what she needs as much as I do."

Levin nodded. "Fuck yes."

He pumped into her, changing his angle and varying the speed and pressure of his pumping until her hands flung outward. She grasped the sheets on one side and

Kon's hand on the other. Her body gathered around him, tensing as he memorized the places she liked him best.

"You're going to come on my dick now, Aven." It wasn't a question. "And this time, I'm going to erupt inside you. I'm going to fill this pussy so full you never forget who it belongs to and whose job it is to take care of it."

Her toes curled where he held her legs in the air. The outcome was inevitable.

Konstantin did his job. He bent down and licked her clit, his tongue also swiping along the topside of Levin's dick as he peeked up with a naughty fucking grin that doomed Levin.

Aven screamed and shattered, her entire being contracting then exploding, surrounding him in the ripples of her ecstasy. There were some things a man simply couldn't resist and the first time he brought his mate to orgasm, buried balls-deep as he realized how profoundly they fit together, was one of them.

Levin roared and drove forward, pistoning within her as Konstantin tipped his face and fused their lips together. He fed Konstantin his groans and Aven his release, shooting deep inside her with spurt after spurt that overflowed her.

And when he finally withdrew, a trickle of his come ran toward her ass.

"No." He pinned her shoulder when she would have moved. "You'll keep every last drop I give you."

He scooped the drip onto his finger and pushed it back inside her. The action only made her shudder some more, causing another rivulet to appear. So he did it again, and again, until she began to settle while holding on to what he'd deposited in her.

When he collapsed to his side next to her,

sandwiching her between him and Kon, she smiled at him up close. So he kissed her then sighed, "You're mine now, little dove, as much as Konstantin is."

"I don't know, you seem to exaggerate." She had the courage to tease him when few people besides Kon ever had before.

"About?" He'd felt how entirely he'd rocked her and knew she had no complaints.

"I thought it was going to last all night?" She sealed her fate by chuckling.

"You think we're done? That was only an appetizer." Levin nuzzled her neck and murmured in her ear. "It's Kon's turn now."

"Oh." Instead of objecting, Aven stretched, reaching for Konstantin and pulling him toward her.

"It is?" Kon lit up, stroking his cock once or twice without permission.

"Yes, and while you fuck her, you're going to suck my cock properly to get it ready for her again. You have to last until I'm hard enough to fuck."

Kon groaned and took his hand away from his dick in a hurry.

"Otherwise, I'm going to spank you next to get it up again." Levin couldn't help the rumble of laughter that rolled through his chest when Konstantin seemed to consider his options and like all of the ones offered.

Levin rolled to his feet, straddling Aven and drew Konstantin's head to his crotch. He used his thumb to pop open Kon's jaw and laid his softened junk on the other man's tongue. "Good boy. Suck and fuck like you know you want to."

Aven hummed when Kon slid home. She'd climaxed twice more by the time Levin stabbed into Kon's throat, fully rejuvenated, inspiring the other man's stride to hitch in Aven's pussy. "Need a break?"

Kon nodded, bobbing his head over Levin's cock.

Levin used his fist in Kon's hair to yank him off his dick, which had liked his man's mouth a little too much to be safe. He shoved Kon to disengage him from Aven when Kon was unable to stop the shuttling of his hips on his own. The man bounced, landing next to her on his side.

"Only for a minute, Kon. I'm going to need your help, remember?" Levin settled onto Aven's other side, ignoring the protest of his ribs when he did. Endorphins were far better than the painkillers he'd refused—believing he deserved to suffer—for masking any discomfort.

He rolled Aven so his cock nestled against her ass. He fucked her crack a few times before reaching between their legs to put himself back inside her. He fit better this time even than the last, his release and Kon's precome easing the way.

Aven tipped her face toward him, her lips parted, and he fulfilled her unspoken request, kissing her until Konstantin's breathing evened out. He asked the man, "Better?"

Konstantin nodded. "She feels so good. It's hard to stop."

"I know. You're doing well." Levin put his thumb in Konstantin's mouth and drew him closer until they could exchange a three-way kiss. Then he growled, "She's ready for us both. I want her to hold us at the same time."

"What?" Aven blinked at him. "Is that possible?"

"You can handle everything we can give you, little dove."

She didn't argue or even flinch, trusting him completely. Levin had won. Right then and there he pledged to all three of them that he would never let them down again.

"You want me to..." Kon verified.

"Yeah." Levin stopped thrusting to give Kon a chance to get settled. "Fuck her with me. Feel her pressing us together, my cock gliding along yours inside her."

"I didn't think you could get any hotter," Konstantin sounded like he'd picked up a two-pack-a-day habit, his voice shredded as he made progress drilling into Aven beside Levin.

"Oh my God." Aven clasped their shoulders. He was sure she would have raked her nails down his back if it hadn't been for his damn healing cuts. There would be time for that later.

She screamed in ecstasy as they stretched her wide.

Levin and Konstantin surrounded Aven. They formed a wall around her that wouldn't let anything through to harm her while stuffing her full of themselves so she couldn't think of anything but the bliss they were bringing her. Levin kissed Konstantin as they fucked her together.

"Your turn, Kon. Unload inside her. Paint us both with your come. Fill her so full it's easy for you to reach when you eat it all out—yours and mine both—while I'm getting my shit together for the next round." Levin had never done something as difficult in his life as keeping himself from orgasming with Konstantin then.

His words alone triggered the rush of seed into Aven's body.

Imagining the mess Konstantin was making of her pussy was enough for her in addition to their pounding cocks, the rub of Konstantin against her clit, and Levin's palm cupping her breast while he bit down on her neck.

Aven joined Kon, coming with the intensity of a sonic boom.

Each time they brought her over the peak was better than the last. Levin became addicted to infusing both of his lovers with boundless pleasure and hoped in time it would erase all of their scars.

If not, he would keep trying until he did.

Levin had found his place and his purpose. If he spent the rest of his life tiring out his two soulmates and making them as happy as possible, it would maybe make up for the things he'd done before he'd known better.

16

A ven floated, completely relaxed, in a wash of pleasure.

"You okay?" Konstantin checked on her as he lay face down on the bed beside her some time later. Had they been at this for hours? She couldn't remember anything from before they'd overloaded her with bliss.

"Feel like I'm flying, but without a plane." She had no idea if she was even making sense anymore.

"You're not afraid?" Kon ran his fingers through her hair as Levin got to his knees, prepared to keep the best night of her life going.

"Nah." There was no fight left in her. She surrendered to the moment and the men who'd made her theirs.

"Which hole should I fuck next?" Levin asked as he regained his footing. He'd already had her jerk him off, iced her chest so Kon could lick it off, and done things to her feet she hadn't known were possible. He stroked his cock as he looked between Aven and Kon's mouths then probed one finger into each of their asses, making her gasp.

But Kon, he shuddered.

"He needs you there." She wondered why Levin hadn't already taken him there when they all knew how much he loved being fucked.

"You sure you don't want to go get your strap-on?" Levin asked her, his jaw clenching at the thought.

"It's fun, but also a lot of work and I need to conserve some energy over here." They were wearing her out. "Unless you're too tired, or...too sore?"

"Does it look like my dick—or any other part of me—has a problem with this? Konstantin can give me one of his incredible massages tomorrow. It'll be fine." Levin could barely wrap his fist around the veiny shaft. "Even if I couldn't get it up right away, I'm not afraid to use your toy myself until both of you have had your fill. You're never going to go to bed disappointed again."

"Okay, so then what's the problem?" Aven asked as Konstantin squirmed, obviously needier than her in that moment.

"Do you have a condom around here? Or could you text one of your friends to bring you some from their stashes?" Levin wondered. "I'm not leaving this bed to go to the damn store and I doubt there's anything open this time of night anyway."

"It's kind of too late to worry about that now, isn't it?" Aven thought of how they'd drenched her repeatedly.

Levin dropped low over her and Konstantin to rasp, "I don't have a single fucking regret about planting my seed in you. I'd love to see you growing with my child—or Kon's—and give you as many ties to us as you want. But I'm not going to risk getting you sick when I want to fuck you again after being buried inside him. Ass to pussy isn't advised and I'm not going to have time to shower every time I want to swap between you two."

Aven shuddered at the thought of them becoming a family, though she needed some time to process a decision as big as that. "Well, for the record, I'm on birth control and Kon's seen me take it every night."

"We can discuss when you'll be stopping that some other time." Levin swiped her phone from the nightstand. "Who's going to hook us up?"

"Try Kennedy." Aven didn't have any hope of forcing her fingers to find tiny buttons right then. "I'm pretty sure she keeps a giant box of them in her store room since she's in charge of health stuff…"

"Perfect."

Kon cursed. "Tell her to hurry, please."

Aven wasn't sure if it was the thought of having a baby together or the promise of Levin's cock stretching his ass open that had him so impatient but either way, it wasn't long before there was a knock at the door along with a sing-songed, "Enjoy!"

Levin sprang from bed and claimed the supplies, donning one before he'd made it back to bed with the whole box and the bottle of lube from her apartment. When he returned, Konstantin rolled on top of her, conducting a study of kissing her well enough to steal every breath.

He rocked against her, his cock sliding against her clit, making her ache to hold him inside her again despite the chain of orgasms they'd already given her.

"That's my boy." Levin patted his ass. "Don't leave Aven out. Give her your cock and I'll give you mine."

Konstantin fit himself into her. He held still, grunting

when Levin bored into him. For a while he lay there and took it, Levin's motions rocking them together and pressing him into her rhythmically. But eventually, he lost his mind, going absolutely wild as he rode her, fucking into her then backing onto Levin's cock on every backstroke.

She was powerless to move or do anything but absorb the reverberations of their passion, and she loved every moment of being used to amplify their pleasure. When Konstantin buckled beneath the double assault of Levin's cock and her pussy, spilling within her, Levin ripped the condom off and took Kon's place, fucking her until she came too.

She had no idea how many different ways they fucked her and each other, in every combination. Slow and deep, fast and frenzied, held together and barely moving, grinding out orgasm after orgasm. One time when they accidentally slipped over the edge together in a chorus of shouts and cries. It was so powerful a release, she thought she might have come hard enough to black out. Her vision went fuzzy on the edges until she realized the difference was actually a subtle orange glow.

"Levin." She dug her nails into his shoulder.

"Just need a minute, and maybe a gallon of water." He raked his teeth over her neck. "It might be time to go find those toys too."

Konstantin groaned, sounding as wrecked as she felt. "I don't think I can do it, Levin. Maybe not for a week at least after this. I haven't come this much since I discovered the internet at the mafia house didn't block gay porn. Fucking hell."

"Guys..." She reached out to each of them, clasping their hands. "Look."

They'd left the curtains wide open so together they turned and took in the strengthening dawn.

"Thank God." Konstantin curled up against her side, hugging her tight, as if she was his own personal teddy bear. "You two wore me out."

From the circle of his arms, she studied Levin, who brushed sweaty locks of her hair from her forehead before propping his shoulders against the headboard. He drew her and Kon's heads onto his lap. "It's a new day, little dove. For all of us."

He'd done as he'd promised and she was certain then that he always would, even if it seemed impossible. No matter how vulnerable she was in their arms, they'd never let loving them hurt her.

Levin had kept his word. He was worthy of her heart, which was good since he'd had it all along.

"You know, don't you?" he asked.

"Know what?" Kon mumbled, as disarmed as she had been.

"That I love you. Both of you," Levin told Aven and Kon, holding each of their gazes as he did. "I'd say I love you enough to kill for you, but I'm not supposed to do shit like that anymore, huh?"

"Only if you do it for the good guys." Aven smiled, sure Levin would fit right in with the rest of the Shields. Which included Konstantin. She looked forward to flying them wherever they needed to go, so long as they all went together. She kissed Levin's thigh and snuggled into Kon's embrace. "I love you too."

"Same. Now can we sleep?" Kon mumbled. "Or better yet, does this place have room service? I could use some breakfast in bed."

"Let me watch the sun come up, then I'll clean you off

and make you *syriniki*." Levin knew exactly what they needed. "Rest. I've got you."

He looked as content as Aven felt right before she closed her eyes, sure he and Konstantin would take good care of her, and each other. It might have taken them longer than they would have liked, but they'd found the perfect place and people to share their future with.

WANT MORE SHIELDS? Click HERE to download a free bonus story. Return to Middletown for another hilarious dose of Aven, Kon, Levin, James and the rest of your favorite Powertools characters! This funny and romantic check in will hold you over until the firefighters of Heat are ready for their spicy adventures to begin.

If you'd like to start at the very beginning of the Powertools world and read more about James and his partners, you can download a discounted boxset of the first six books HERE.

Yes, I know it says complete series but I wrote a seventh book more recently and haven't gotten around to updating the boxset yet, sorry!

You can find the seventh Powertools book, More the Merrier, HERE.

They are also featured in four books in the Powertools: The Original Crew Returns series starting with Screwed HERE

To read more about the Hot Rides gang—where you'll find Jordan, Wren, and Kason's full story—start with Quinn, Trevon, and Devra's book, Wild Ride, click HERE.

If you missed out on the Powertools: Hot Rods series, you can buy all eight books in a discounted single-volume boxset by clicking HERE.

Did you know Jayne brought the original Powertools crew back for four more books? Click HERE to get caught up.

CLAIM A $5 GIFT CERTIFICATE

Jayne is so sure you will love her books, she'd like you to try any one of your choosing for free. Claim your $5 gift certificate by signing up for her newsletter. You'll also learn about freebies, new releases, extras, appearances, and more!

www.jaynerylon.com/newsletter

WHAT WAS YOUR FAVORITE PART?

Did you enjoy this book? If so, please leave a review and tell your friends about it. Word of mouth and online reviews are immensely helpful and greatly appreciated.

JAYNE'S SHOP

Check out Jayne's online shop for autographed print
books, direct download ebooks, reading-themed apparel
up to size 5XL, mugs, tote bags, notebooks, Mr. Rylon's
wood (you'll have to see it for yourself!) and more.
www.jaynerylon.com/shop

LISTEN UP!

The majority of Jayne's books are also available in audio format on Audible, Amazon and iTunes.

ABOUT THE AUTHOR

Jayne Rylon is a New York Times and USA Today bestselling author, who has sold more than two million copies of her books. She has received numerous industry awards including the Romantic Times Reviewers' Choice Award for Best Indie Erotic Romance and the Swirl Award, which recognizes excellence in diverse romance. She is an Honor Roll member of the Romance Writers of America. Her stories used to begin as daydreams in seemingly endless business meetings, but now she is a full time author, who employs the skills she learned from her straight-laced corporate existence in the business of writing. She lives in Ohio with her husband, the infamous Mr. Rylon, and kittens they foster for a rescue organization. When she can escape her purple office, she loves to travel the world, avoid speeding tickets in her beloved Sky, SCUBA dive, and–of course–read.

Jayne Loves To Hear From Readers
www.jaynerylon.com
contact@jaynerylon.com
PO Box 10, Pickerington, OH 43147

You can find her on TikTok making a fool of herself at @jaynerylon

facebook.com/jaynerylon

twitter.com/JayneRylon

instagram.com/jaynerylon

youtube.com/jaynerylonbooks

bookbub.com/profile/jayne-rylon

amazon.com/author/jaynerylon

ALSO BY JAYNE RYLON

4-EVER

A New Adult Reverse Harem Series

4-Ever Theirs

4-Ever Mine

EVER AFTER DUET

Reverse Harem Featuring Characters From The 4-Ever Series

Fourplay

Fourkeeps

EVER & ALWAYS DUET

Reverse Harem Featuring Characters from the 4-Ever and Ever After Duets

Four Money

Four Love

POWERTOOLS: THE ORIGINAL CREW

Five Guys Who Get It On With Each Other & One Girl. Enough Said?

Kate's Crew

Morgan's Surprise

Kayla's Gift

Devon's Pair

Nailed to the Wall

Hammer it Home

More the Merrier *NEW*

POWERTOOLS: HOT RODS

Powertools Spin Off. Keep up with the Crew plus...

Seven Guys & One Girl. Enough Said?

King Cobra

Mustang Sally

Super Nova

Rebel on the Run

Swinger Style

Barracuda's Heart

Touch of Amber

Long Time Coming

POWERTOOLS: HOT RIDES

Powertools and Hot Rods Spin Off.

Menage and Motorcycles

Wild Ride

Slow Ride

Hard Ride

Joy Ride

Rough Ride

POWERTOOLS: RETURN OF THE CREW

The original crew is back with more steamy menage stories!

Screwed

Drilled

Grind

Pound

POWERTOOLS: THE SHIELDS

Do-gooder Polyamorous Assassins in MMF Menages

Found

Lost

Brazen

Broken

Claimed

Shared

POWERTOOLS: HEAT

Coming Soon

MEN IN BLUE

Hot Cops Save Women In Danger

Night is Darkest

Razor's Edge

Mistress's Master

Spread Your Wings

Wounded Hearts

Bound For You

DIVEMASTERS

Sexy SCUBA Instructors By Day, Doms On A Mega-Yacht By Night

Going Down

Going Deep

Going Hard

STANDALONE

Menage

Middleman

Nice & Naughty

Contemporary

Where There's Smoke

Report For Booty

COMPASS BROTHERS

Modern Western Family Drama Plus Lots Of Steamy Sex

Northern Exposure

Southern Comfort

Eastern Ambitions

Western Ties

COMPASS GIRLS

Daughters Of The Compass Brothers Drive Their Dads Crazy And Fall In Love

Winter's Thaw

Hope Springs

Summer Fling

Falling Softly

COMPASS BOYS

Sons Of The Compass Brothers Fall In Love

Heaven on Earth

Into the Fire

Still Waters

Light as Air

PLAY DOCTOR

Naughty Sexual Psychology Experiments Anyone?

Dream Machine

Healing Touch

RED LIGHT

A Hooker Who Loves Her Job

Complete Red Light Series Boxset

FREE - Through My Window - FREE

Star

Can't Buy Love

Free For All

PICK YOUR PLEASURES

Choose Your Own Adventure Romances!

Pick Your Pleasure

Pick Your Pleasure 2

RACING FOR LOVE

MMF Menages With Race-Car Driver Heroes

Complete Series Boxset

Driven

Shifting Gears

PARANORMALS

Vampires, Witches, And A Man Trapped In A Painting

Paranormal Double Pack Boxset

Picture Perfect

Reborn

PENTHOUSE PLEASURES
Naughty Manhattanite Neighbors Find Kinky Love

Taboo

Kinky

Sinner

Mentor

ROAMING WITH THE RYLONS
Non-fiction Travelogues about Jayne & Mr. Rylon's Adventures

Australia and New Zealand

www.ingramcontent.com/pod-product-compliance
Lightning Source LLC
Chambersburg PA
CBHW051044050726
47592CB00002B/380